Riley Mae
and the
Ready Eddy Rapids

Also by Jill Osborne

Riley Mae and the Rock Shocker Trek

Other books in the growing Faithgirlz!™ library

Bibles

The Faithgirlz! Bible
NIV Faithgirlz! Backpack Bible

Faithgirlz! Bible Studies

Secret Power of Love
Secret Power of Joy
Secret Power of Goodness
Secret Power of Grace

Fiction

From Sadie's Sketchbook

Shades of Truth (Book One)
Flickering Hope (Book Two)
Waves of Light (Book Three)
Brilliant Hues (Book Four)

Sophie's World Series

Meet Sophie (Book One)
Sophie Steps Up (Book Two)
Sophie and Friends (Book Three)
Sophie's Friendship Fiasco (Book Four)
Sophie Flakes Out (Book Five)
Sophie's Drama (Book Six)

The Lucy Series

Lucy Doesn't Wear Pink (Book One)
Lucy Out of Bounds (Book Two)
Lucy's Perfect Summer (Book Three)
Lucy Finds Her Way (Book Four)

The Girls of Harbor View

Girl Power (Book One)
Take Charge (Book Two)
Raising Faith (Book Three)
Secret Admirer (Book Four)

Boarding School Mysteries

Vanished (Book One)
Betrayed (Book Two)
Burned (Book Three)
Poisoned (Book Four)

Nonfiction

Faithgirlz Handbook
Faithgirlz Journal
Food, Faith, and Fun! Faithgirlz Cookbook
Real Girls of the Bible
My Beautiful Daughter
You! A Christian Girl's Guide to Growing Up
Girl Politics
Everybody Tells Me to Be Myself, but I Don't Know Who I Am

Devotions for Girls Series

No Boys Allowed

What's a Girl to Do?

Girlz Rock

Chick Chat

Shine On, Girl!

Check out www.faithgirlz.com

The Good News Shoes

Riley Mae
and the
Ready Eddy Rapids

BOOK TWO

Jill Osborne

ZONDERKIDZ

Riley Mae and the Ready Eddy Rapids

Copyright © 2013 by Jill Osborne

This title is also available as a Zondervan ebook.
Visit www.zondervan.com/ebooks

Requests for information should be addressed to:
Zonderkidz, 3900 Sparks Drive, Grand Rapids, Michigan 49546

978-0-310-74299-9

Editor: Kim Childress
Art direction: Deborah Washington
Cover design and interior decoration: Jennifer Zivoin
Interior design: Ben Fetterley and Greg Johnson
Interior composition: Greg Johnson/Textbook Perfect

Printed in the United States of America

HB 11.09.2017

To Jared and Pam—
For your unwavering friendship
and for making it your mission to provide us
with opportunities for fun and adventure,
including that rafting trip
where Jesus took the wheel.

"For shoes, put on the peace that
comes from the Good News
so that you will be fully prepared."

EPHESIANS 6:15 NLT

Chapter 1

Running for your life is not as exciting as it looks in the movies. And it's not something I ever expected to do, especially since I'm only twelve. Well, almost thirteen, but that doesn't make it any better. I never thought that being the spokesgirl for the Riley Mae Outdoor Shoe Collection would totally mess up my life. I suppose if I *had* thought about it a little more carefully, I would not have begged my parents to sign that rotten two-year contract. Mom always says that I "fail to think things through." But this time, I really tried! I *thought* it would be fun to be famous. I *thought* it would be great to wear new shoes all the time. I *thought* it would be interesting to travel to new places. But even in a million years I *never* would have thought it would get me in this much trouble!

"So, your *real* name is Daniel Stevens?" I squinted at the guy sitting across the aisle from me in the private jet. Just a day ago, I thought his name was Flip Miller, my silly photographer from Swiftriver shoes—a guy who wears wrinkly clothes and eats stale leftovers from his pants pockets.

"Yeah, but you can still call me Flip."

"And you're rich?"

He pushed his cushy seat back into a reclining position. "I guess you could say that."

"And that's why you can sponsor all those kids from other countries, right? It all makes sense now."

Flip grinned. "My dad always sponsored kids when I was little. I thought it was cool. I wrote them letters and sent toys whenever I could. When I got old enough to sponsor a kid on my own, it was hard to pick just one, so I figured, why not? I can afford a few more."

"Yeah, but when TJ and I visited your office—"

"You mean when you broke into my office—"

I looked over at my dad, who was snoozing in the seat next to me. I never told him about that time when TJ's older sister Breanne took us to Flip's office to spy on him.

"Okay," I whispered. "When we 'broke in,' we saw pictures of TWO HUNDRED sponsored kids on your wall."

"Like I said, it was hard to pick."

The woman sitting next to Flip—the person I had known as Fawn, my bossy personal assistant at Swiftriver shoes—spoke up.

"I always remember Dad saying that God cares more about what we give than what we have."

Flip's and Fawn's dad was some guy named Drake Stevens, a famous millionaire and real estate developer from New York. I say *was*, because he's dead now. He was killed by some nasty people in his own company, who I guess wanted his money. If he was as generous as Flip says he was, why didn't they just ask him for the money? No need to kill the guy.

I turned my suspicious glance toward Fawn.

"And *your* real name is Samantha Stevens? Sister of ... *him?* I raised my eyebrows and pointed to Flip.

"Shocking, I know," Flip said, as he ran his fingers through his dark brown, perfect-model hair. "I'm sure you're thinking, 'How did the brother get all the brains and charm, leaving his poor sister with nothing but a bad temper and a horrible taste in clothing?'"

"No," Fawn said, "I'm sure Riley was wondering how I've managed to put up with such a goofball for a little brother all my life. Isn't that right, Riley?"

"You guys are starting to sound like me and Brady." (Brady's *my* little brother, who's not so much a goofball, but a genius who sometimes—okay, lots of times—gets on my nerves.)

"So," I continued, "you changed your identities to escape the bad guys. I get that. But then you moved to Fresno? To start an outdoor shoe company? Why?"

Fawn shrugged. "Because we like adventure."

She hardly got those words out of her mouth when

the plane jolted—hard. My lemonade glass flew off the tray in front of me and spilled out onto my shoes. Great, that would leave a sticky mess. Good thing I had about a hundred backup pairs in my luggage.

Flip straightened his chair and buckled his seat belt, then yelled up to our pilot. "What happened, Tyler? You just clip a mountain or somethin'?"

"No," Tyler yelled back. "Just some turbulence. Everything's under control." I couldn't see Tyler's face, but he sounded calm.

The plane bumped again. Good thing there was nothing left to spill. My dad, who was now awake and reading a fishing magazine, had a concerned look on his face.

"Flip, how well do you know this pilot?"

"I know what you're thinking, Mr. Hart, and you can relax. I've known Tyler for a long time. He'd never sell us out."

"What's that mean?" I asked.

"It means we can trust him to keep us safe," Dad said.

I looked out the window of the plane and tried to guess where we were. No clues yet, since we were above clouds.

"Why can't you guys tell me where we're going? It's not like I can tell anyone, since you took my phone."

"That was just a protective measure," Dad said.

The plane dipped and bumped again. I grabbed my armrest.

Eric Stevens, Flip's and Fawn's younger half brother, stumbled down the aisle from the bathroom. "Nice bump." He rubbed his lip. "I think I chipped a tooth in there."

"How come no one's after *you?*" I asked him. As far as I knew, only Flip and Fawn had been hiding undercover as Swiftriver shoe employees. "Don't you like adventure?"

"Sure. I've been experiencing lots of it trying to find these guys." He pointed to Flip and Fawn and then took a seat and buckled up.

"Are you rich too?"

Eric grinned and nodded. "Dad made sure we were well taken care of after the divorce. He loved my mom a lot. She loved him too, but she couldn't take the heat of being Drake Stevens' wife. Too many people use you for your money."

"And want you dead." I wished I hadn't said that when I saw Fawn frown and look down.

"I'm sorry, Fawn."

"That's okay." She looked back up and half smiled.

This all was so crazy. I had been working with Flip and Fawn for six months, but now I felt like I had to get to know them all over again.

For example, Fawn had on a new pair of Riley Mae Rock Shocker hiking boots—which was a whole lot different than those fancy high heels she'd been wearing over the last few months.

"So," I said, "the 'real' Fawn likes sports." I pointed to her boots. "Do you have a favorite sport?"

She didn't even have to think. "Running. I like breathing hard. It makes me feel alive."

Huh. That was interesting. "My softball coach sometimes makes us run a mile before practice. It makes me feel like I'm gonna die."

Fawn laughed. "I joined our school's cross-country team when I was in fourth grade. The first time I ran a mile, I felt the same way. My mom was a runner, so she encouraged me to keep going."

"I thought your mom died a long time ago."

I felt bad as soon as I mentioned that. Sometimes I think it would be helpful for me to put some sparkly pink duct tape over my lips and leave it there for good.

Fawn didn't seem too disturbed. "She died of breast cancer that same year, when I was nine. After that, I decided I'd always keep running, kind of as a special way to remember her."

"Did it get easier?"

Fawn's eyes narrowed. "Did *what* get easier?"

"The running, I mean."

"Oh … no. It's not supposed to get easier. You always want to increase your mileage or your speed."

"Yikes. I better not take up running then."

Fawn gave me a confused look. "No, it's really a great thing to do. You would love it, Riley, and since you're a spokesgirl for athletic shoes, you should know a little about every sport." She looked around for a minute. "I've got a running magazine around here somewhere. Hang on …"

Fawn got up and searched through some of her tote bags. She eventually pulled out a magazine with a runner on the front cover and started flipping through it. Then she settled back in a chair, smiled, and began reading.

I glanced over at Flip, who was sitting across the aisle. "I guess she forgot about me."

Flip looked in his sister's direction. "She does that to me all the time. She'll come back around." He pulled a deck of cards out of his backpack. "Wanna play Go Fish?"

I sighed. "That's the most boring game in the universe."

"Nah! We can pep it up. How about we put the cards in a bowl under a bunch of goldfish crackers, and then when you go fish, you have to stick your face in and pull out a card?"

Well, at least *that* sounded like the Flip I knew.

"Interesting, but … I'd have to have my own cards and bowl. I'm not sticking my face anywhere you've stuck your face."

"Good point." Flip shuffled the cards and looked disappointed. "Sorry. Only one deck."

I tapped my chin with my fingers. "Hmmm. How about we have Eric hide the cards, and then when we have to go fish, we go on a search and we don't come back till we have a match?"

Flip shook his head. "Good idea, but I have this, remember?" Flip lifted up his right foot, which was wrapped in a cast. Was that just a few days ago when he broke his ankle practically falling off Half Dome in Yosemite?

"Yeah," I said. "Guess that won't work either." Then I remembered that I had a softball with me.

"I know! Let's play Manly Sting." I pulled the pink and purple colored ball out of my backpack, tossed it up in the air, and caught it.

My dad dropped his magazine and held up a hand. "Don't do it, Flip."

Flip laughed. "Seriously? Why not?"

"Because it's dangerous!"

I punched Dad in the arm. "It is not! You were the one who taught it to me."

"And you got way too good at it."

I smiled and tossed the ball up again.

"I wanna play!" Flip reached over and caught the ball as it came down.

"Okay." I swiveled my fancy jet chair to face the aisle, a few feet from Flip. "This is what you do. Throw the ball as hard as you can, and I have to catch it with my bare hand, without making any sound."

"Are you kidding? It'll tear your arm off!"

"No it won't, because the rule is, you can't wind up. You have to keep your arm still and only use wrist snap." I grabbed the ball from Flip to demonstrate, but without throwing the ball. "The first one to make any noise when they catch the ball loses."

"Sounds easy to me," Flip said.

My dad shook his head and then covered his eyes. "I can't watch this."

I handed the ball back to Flip. "Okay, then, you throw first." I held up my empty hand and waited to absorb the sting of the ball. But when Flip released the ball, it dribbled straight down his arm and onto the floor. Then it rolled up to the front of the plane.

"Woops." He lifted his cast again. "Guess you have to be the gofer for this game."

I retrieved the ball and returned to my seat. "You ready?"

"Bring it on!" Flip held up his hand.

I snapped the ball toward him, and he caught it. "Yeeeeeeouuuuuuuuch!"

"I told you," Dad said. "She's been working on that wrist snap for five years."

Flip shook his hand out. "Okay, I get it now. I wasn't ready for that. Let's play again."

"No problem." I held my empty hand up again. "Throw away."

Flip snapped the ball and this time it reached the target. It stung a little, but I remained silent. After many years of playing Manly Sting, I've trained myself to say "oww" in my head.

"Okay, my throw. You ready this time?"

Flip rubbed his hands together and leaned forward. "Let's go!"

I snapped the ball again, this time a little harder.

A funny grunt came from Flip's neck area.

I giggled. "That was a throat yelp."

"It was barely a noise!"

"*Any* noise counts. Now you throw. If I don't make a noise, I win again."

Flip practiced snapping his wrist a few times. "Okay, get ready. This is going to be super manly."

He wasn't kidding. He hurled it in. When it hit my hand I flinched a little, and the sting made my eyes water. That time, I said "WAAAAAAHHHHH" in my head. The only person who had ever thrown me one harder than that was my best friend, TJ, and she's the number one pitcher in our league.

Flip looked at me with wide eyes. "Uh-oh. I better quit while *you're* ahead."

"I told you," Dad said again.

Chapter 2

"Hey, anyone want a snack? This manly sting stuff is making me hungry." Flip got up and tripped a little trying to walk in his ankle cast.

"Sit down, dummy." Fawn jumped up from reading her magazine and passed Flip in the aisle. "I'll get your food. You also have a concussion, remember?"

"Oh yeah. Riley, *that* must be why I lost."

"Are you even supposed to be flying?" Dad asked Flip.

Flip sat back down and rubbed his head. "Doesn't matter, does it? Anyway, we'll be landing in an hour or so."

Ah, a clue! I checked my watch. I wished I had paid attention to the time when we took off. Rats. We had to have been in the air at least an hour. How far could we get from California in two hours? And what direction were we flying?

My brother Brady would know. That kid can pick up a blank piece of paper and draw the whole United States in about three minutes—disgusting. Too bad he wasn't here. The lucky duck was staying with my grandparents for a few days while Mom worked on investigating the Swiftriver mess.

My mom's the chief of police in Clovis. That's a city right next to where we live in Fresno, California. She was the one who figured out that Flip and Fawn weren't really Flip and Fawn. She's suspicious of everyone, which used to bug me, but considering I'm on the run with people who are being hunted down by bad guys, I guess that's a good thing now.

Fawn returned with a plate of fruit and a big bowl of goldfish crackers. I grabbed a handful real quick, just in case Flip was tempted to stick his face in.

"So, what's your 'secret' cabin like?" I asked. "Will I have to sleep on the floor in a sleeping bag?"

Flip laughed so hard that a goldfish cracker flew out of his mouth. He caught it in the air. "Our cabin is ... well, I guess calling it a cabin is a little deceiving. It's more like—"

"A resort." Eric reached over to the fruit plate and snatched up some grapes. "I'm pretty sure you can see the place from outer space it's so big."

"I love that place." Fawn closed her eyes. "It's so peaceful by the lake."

"You have your own lake?" I elbowed Dad, who was reading his magazine again. "Did you hear that, Dad?"

"Well, it's a small lake," Eric said. "But you can still take a boat out—"

"A boat?" Dad got all excited. "Is it, by chance, a *fishing* boat?"

"We have a lot of boats," Eric said. "Fishing boats, ski boats, row boats, kayaks—"

"Wow," Dad's eyes got wide. "I may never go back to work."

That started a really boring conversation between Eric and my dad about fishing. The plane bumped again, so I buckled my seat belt. Great—no escape. I had no choice but to rest my head on my pillow, close my eyes, and pretend I was on a roller coaster.

I guess I fell asleep, but I'm not sure for how long.

"Riley." Dad shook me. He grabbed my seat belt and pulled. "Are you all buckled in? We're landing."

I had to think about where I was for a minute. Oh, yeah. I had no idea. I looked out the window. Maybe there would be a clue now. This time I saw bunches of trees and mountains in the distance. Tall ones, some covered in snow.

I rubbed my eyes. "Are we in Alaska?"

"Good guess, but no," Fawn said.

We flew over a lake, and I wondered if it was the Stevens's secret resort lake. The ground came up quickly, and I heard a jolt underneath the plane. The landing gear coming down made me jump, but then when I remembered what the noise was all about, I relaxed back into my seat.

That's when the plane rose back up.

"How come we're not going down?" I asked.

Flip looked confused. "Not sure. Hang on ..."

He got up and limped to the front of the plane. Fawn didn't stop him this time. He disappeared into the cockpit as the plane rose even higher in the air.

"Maybe Tyler got his states mixed up," Eric said.

A couple minutes later, Flip returned, with a fake grin on his face. "Anyone got a parachute? Our landing gear's busted."

"Don't even joke about that," Fawn said.

"I'm not joking. The right wheel won't come down. Tyler's going to fly around a little and try to fix it."

My head started pounding. "How's he gonna do that?"

"Oh, it's an easy fix. He just needs to climb out the front window and swing down there and pull it out. Should only take a minute."

I must have looked panicked, because Eric got up off his seat to come over to pat me on the shoulder.

"That's not the real plan. Flip's always been a kidder." He turned to look at his older brother. "What's he really gonna do, bro?" Eric was breathing a little hard, and he kept flipping his head to the side to keep his blond, curly bangs out of his eyes.

Next, Dad got up and went into the cockpit. That

made me nervous. He came back in a couple of minutes, looking very concerned. "Okay, gang. Here's the plan. Tyler's going to run the plane out of fuel, and if the landing gear hasn't righted itself by then, he'll land on the front and left wheels."

"Why do we have to run the plane out of gas? Won't we crash?" I grabbed my pillow and squeezed.

"Oh, we're definitely going to crash. We just don't want to blow up. Right, Mr. Hart?" Flip threw a grape in the air and caught it in his mouth.

"Flip! Will you just stop? Haven't we had enough drama in the last week?" Fawn grabbed the grapes from Flip, and a few bounced down the aisle.

Eric was the next one to visit the cockpit. Maybe he'd come back with a better story.

Nope.

"He can't fix it," Eric said. "So, he's going to let her down ... gently."

"A soft crash. I like that. Better than Half Dome, right kiddo?" Flip reached over and flicked my arm.

"Dad, can I go talk to Tyler?" I needed to do something to keep the adrenaline from squirting out of my ears.

"No, you just stay put."

"Can I go to the bathroom?"

"Do you really have to go?"

"I'm not sure, but I don't want to wet my pants during

the crash." I couldn't believe I was even saying the *word* crash. We weren't *really going to crash*, right?

Next, Fawn got up. It wasn't fair that *everyone* had been up but me, so I escaped before Dad could stop me. I followed Fawn into the cockpit.

"Hi, ladies. How's your afternoon going?" Funny. Tyler didn't look nervous at all.

Fawn got right to the point. "Are we going to crash?"

Tyler shook his head. "Oh, no. I've had this happen tons of times."

"Really?" That made me feel better.

"Well, it was on a simulator, but each time I landed my plane with just a tiny scratch."

"Wait," I said. "Isn't a simulator a practice thing?"

Fawn pushed me out of the cockpit. "He's got this under control. Let's go get buckled up and ready for our 'tiny scratch' landing."

We hurried back, shoved all our stuff under the seats, and piled pillows in our laps.

Dad had his Bible open. "Hey Riley, listen to this. Remember the 9-1-1 Scripture?"

Uh-oh. Dad only saves that Bible passage for super scary situations.

Dad began reading from Psalm 91, verses 1–2:

"The person who rests in the shadow of the Most High God will be kept safe by the Mighty One. I will say about the Lord, *'He is like a fort to me. He is my God. I trust in him ...'"*

Dad put his hand on my back and kept reading, and that's when I got really nervous. I tried to listen to my favorite parts of the psalm—about being covered with feathers and about God ordering angels to protect you wherever you go. I thought back to the worst crash I'd ever been in. It was when I was riding my bike a couple of years ago. I had turned around to say something to TJ, and I ran into a parked car. My bike got mangled, and I ended up with a huge headache and a hundred little cuts all over my body. It was horrible. But at least I didn't *know* it was coming.

A few minutes later, the ground got closer again. I heard Tyler yell, "Here we go, everyone hold on!" I wish I didn't know *this* was coming.

Chapter 3

Dad threw his arm over in front of me, like he was trying to hold me with all his strength in my seat. I shoved my face into the pile of pillows. I closed my eyes tight, and all I could picture was that mangled bike.

I waited for a huge thump, but it didn't come. I felt the plane touch down on the left wheel, and I heard the brakes take hold, but we stayed smooth. I could tell the tip of the jet was still up. I hoped we were on a long runway, because Tyler was sure taking his time setting down that front wheel. Finally he did it, but instead of feeling the bump, skid, and crash I expected, I just felt a bump, a tip, and a scrape. And then we came to a stop, only we weren't straight. It was kind of like when my dad raised my training wheels when I was a little kid, and I tipped and got stuck, leaning to the right, but I didn't fall.

"Is that it? Are we done?" I looked up, but all I saw was balled-up people.

Fawn lifted her head and glanced from side to side. "What do we do now?"

"Hey," Flip said, "I think we finally get to use that blow-up escape slide!"

"Ooh—I'll get it ready!" Eric unbuckled himself and popped into action. He had the emergency exit door opened and the escape slide ready to go in seconds.

"Ladies, first!"

Eric held his hand out to me.

"Wait, I need to grab my stuff."

"Later," Dad said. "For now, let's just get out of this tube."

So Fawn and I slid out first. I felt a little silly, since it wasn't a massive plane wreck or anything. As we came down the slide, I noticed that several emergency crews had arrived. Some firemen helped us off at the bottom and offered to take us over to the paramedic truck to get checked out. One of them motioned to the big bandage on Fawn's leg, which covered the gash she got when she slid her shin down the sharp granite on the Half Dome hike.

"Oh, that's from my last crash," Fawn said, and her cheeks turned a little red.

This was shaping up to be quite a week.

Dad and Eric slid out next, followed by Flip in his cast. He came down head first.

Fawn got mad about that. "Is your brain numb, or what?"

"I guess," Flip said. "My ankle hurts worse than my head. I didn't want to bump it."

"Where's Tyler?" Dad asked. "I need to thank him. That landing was smoother than most I've experienced on fully functioning landing gear."

We all watched as Tyler flew down the slide. He started with a handstand at the top, which turned into a front somersault, and then he popped off at the bottom and landed on his feet. He brushed the dust off his pilot's jacket and shook each of our hands. "Good job, crew. I told you this was only going to be a scratch landing."

"That was amazing! How'd you do it? Weren't you scared?" I was feeling pretty energetic all of a sudden—kind of like I just ate two chocolate donuts.

"Concerned, but not scared," Tyler said. Then he turned to Flip. "We need to have a serious talk though. I checked that plane out thoroughly this morning. Everything was fine. Equipment doesn't just break down like that."

"Are you saying someone messed with the landing gear?" Flip walked closer to the plane and tried to poke his head under where the right wheel should have been.

"Don't know, but I can't wait to hoist this baby up and have one of our mechanics take a look." Tyler rubbed his hand across the tip of the wing. "For now, it looks like I need to get out the backup jet."

"You have two of these things?" I said. "Wow. You people *are* rich."

A big, black SUV pulled up on the runway, and a really tall cowboy got out. The hat, boots, and shiny belt buckle gave that away.

"Howdy, Big Chuck!" Eric jogged over to the cowboy and slapped him on the back.

"Well, if it ain't the youngest Stevens kid!" The cowboy shook Eric's hand. "Lessee, you gotta be at least twenty or so by now if I got my math right."

"That's exactly right. Wow—Chuck, it's been a long time."

"Too long if ya ask me."

Flip and Fawn brought me and Dad over to meet the sandy-haired cowboy.

"This is our good friend, Chuck Edwards," Flip said. "But we just call him Big Chuck. Or sometimes, Lucky Chuck." Flip gave Chuck a big hug. "Chuck taught me how to ride a horse."

Chuck knelt down and examined Flip's ankle cast. "Looks like you fell off one, Son."

"Close. About fell off the saddle of Half Dome."

I shivered remembering that again.

"Wooooooeeeeeee! I'd say I should be calling you 'lucky' now!" Chuck walked over and opened all the doors to the SUV. "I reckon y'all wanna be gettin' home?"

Fawn jumped in the back seat. "You bet. Can't wait to go sit in the hot tub. It's been a long two years."

"Well, it's about time you came back around. Wait till

you see the place. Carmie's got the flowers blooming all beeeaaauuutiful-like!"

Chuck helped me up the big step and into the back of the SUV. "Ladies as pretty as you two must have come with a little luggage. Where's it all at?"

Fawn pointed to the tilting plane. "We'll have it sent later. Right now we just want to get off this runway."

Chuck winked. "Gotcha."

The men all piled in after us—except Tyler, who said he wanted to stay back to help the mechanic inspect the plane problems. They barely got the doors closed before Chuck peeled out of there. I tried to see some signs of where we might be, but the car was going too fast, and the tinted windows in the back were really dark. It felt like we were in a car chase with the way Chuck was squealing around the corners.

"I see you still like speed," Eric told Chuck.

Chuck laughed. "No sense wasting time in a car when perfectly good horses are waitin'."

Fawn grabbed her stomach. "Can you slow it down a little so the people in the back don't end up si—"

BANG!

The back of the SUV sank and jerked to the right side. Fawn and I screamed. I also ducked and covered my head because it sounded like a gun just went off.

Chapter 4

"Whoa, Nellie!" Chuck swung the steering wheel in different directions while the car spun around a couple of times. A loud squeal sounded from my side of the car, and my seat belt locked and dug into my shoulder. For a minute all I could see was a blur of stuff, since my head was being whipped from side to side. Then my side of the car hit something hard and my head smacked up against the window, squishing my ear. Ouch. Whatever we hit stopped us. Whew.

It was too quiet in the car. I rubbed my ear and looked around, expecting to see everyone dead. Thankfully, they weren't. But they moved in slow motion, unbuckling their seat belts and opening doors.

"What happened? Was someone shooting at us?" I tried to catch my breath, but it felt like someone was standing on my chest. I looked down to make sure there was no gunshot wound. No blood. Huh. Maybe the shooter missed. I looked out the window to the right and spied a huge tree next to the SUV. Yep, that's what we hit.

Chuck leaped out the door and came around the outside of my window.

"That, little lady, was a big-ol' blowout. Wooooooo-eeeeee! That was rowdy!" He bent down to where I couldn't see him anymore, and then came back up, scratching his head. "The damage isn't too bad," he said to all the guys, who were now standing by him, leaning against the tree.

Dad opened the driver's side door, and climbed back to where Fawn and I were. "You okay, Honey?"

I grabbed my chest.

"I can't breathe." It felt like I was trying to suck air through a plugged straw.

Dad helped me unbuckle my seat belt and pulled me out of the car onto the side of the road. "There, now you have some fresh air. Sit down a minute."

I did, and I was immediately poked by pine needles. "Ouch." I jumped back up. "Dad, I wanna go home."

"Don't we all," Fawn said.

I started to cry. I hated that. I'm not usually a cry baby. And this was the third or fourth time in a couple of days when I couldn't control the tears flying out. That didn't help with my breathing either.

Dad picked me up like I was a little kid, and I wrapped my arms around his neck. I wiped my tears on his shirt and let my legs dangle for a couple of minutes. Then the guys came back around to my side of the car.

"What's all the ruckus?" Chuck asked. "It's a flat tire, that's all. There's barely a dent in the side. We'll be outta here in no time."

"I think she's having a little meltdown," Fawn said. "It's been a stressful week."

Dad stood me up on my feet, and Flip patted me on the shoulder. "Looks like you need a Samantha Special."

"Ooooh, yes!" Fawn clapped her hands really fast. "That's EXACTLY what we all need."

"Well, okay then," Chuck said. "Let's get this horsey movin'!"

The men flew into action—except Flip, who had that cast. He just stood there and grinned at me funny. We both watched as they pulled everything apart and came up with a spare tire and some tools to crank the car up. My head felt dizzy, but at least I wasn't struggling to get a breath anymore. As I started to come to my senses, I looked around for a mirror. The only one I could find was the one sticking out of the side of the car on the driver's side. I never should have looked in it, because I was horrified to see how my light-brown waves had turned all frizzy and my skin was red under my right eye. That always happens when I cry, and it takes forever for it to go away.

Fawn came to the rescue and pulled my hair up with an elastic band.

"There, that's better," she said. "Gotta love ponytails."

"What's a Samantha Special?"

"Something you're gonna love." Fawn smiled and rubbed her stomach.

Chapter 5

The men changed that tire super fast, and before I was ready, I was strapped back in my seat again. Chuck peeled out, whipped a U-turn and headed back in the direction of the airport.

"Samantha Special, comin' right up!"

We drove for about five minutes, and as we passed the airport, this time I noticed the sign: *Glacier International Airport*. I started wondering again if we were in Alaska. Then we turned into a Dairy Queen parking lot. I really hoped that had something to do with the Samantha Special.

"You stay here, Riley," Flip said. "Gotta keep our location secret for a couple more days. I don't want you asking any questions."

Fawn noticed my frown and whispered in my ear. "Don't worry, it'll be worth the wait."

They all went into the Dairy Queen and left me in the car to do some snooping. This would be a breeze, figuring out where we were. I'm not a Nancy Drew fan for nothing. What *would* Nancy do? I looked through the window of the Dairy Queen and noticed that our group was already ordering. Nancy would hurry up, that's what.

I thought about getting out of the car, but I saw Flip watching out the window. Rats. Better stay in. No problem—the scenery would give me some clues. First I checked for road signs. I couldn't see any, except two on the corner that said First and Spruce. No help there. It would have been great if I'd seen a sign that said, "Welcome to Colorado or Welcome to Arizona," although I figured by all the towering mountain peaks that we weren't in Arizona. I also remembered the flight to Arizona being much shorter than the one we took here. But maybe Colorado . . .

Just then, a semitruck drove into the parking lot with a Colorado license plate. Yep, that's what I thought! That would make sense. I sat back in my seat and grinned at my cleverness. I couldn't wait to inform my group that they couldn't fool Riley Mae Hart. I looked back through the Dairy Queen window just as an employee was handing an ice cream cone to my dad. Yum. I hoped that was the Samantha Special. Another car zoomed into the parking lot—this one with an Idaho license plate. The motorcycle that followed in behind it had an Alberta license plate. Isn't Alberta in Canada? Great, this strategy wasn't working. I wanted to get out of the car and look at the license plate of Chuck's car, but—there was Flip, still staring out the window.

Think, Riley. What can you find in the car?

I looked all around, but Chuck's car was the cleanest I'd ever been in. Not even a paper scrap anywhere. But there was a glove compartment. I crawled over the seats for what seemed like a mile, and I stretched my hand out to pull the lever to open it. I expected a ton of junk to fall out—like what happens when we open the one in our minivan. But Chuck's was practically empty. Only two things were in there. A thick book of some kind and another piece of paper. My parents keep a registration slip hidden in all the junk in our glove compartment. I hoped that's what this paper was.

"Whatcha doin' up here, kiddo? I thought you were too busy having a stress attack to snoop." Flip stared at me from outside the passenger side window, drinking something, but it looked like he was having trouble with his straw. His lips were all puckered up, and his cheeks were sinking in. He finally gave up.

"Aww, I need a spoon." He turned to go back inside the Dairy Queen. I reached for the paper with one hand while keeping both eyes on him. I just needed one second to look to see if it was the registration ...

"Got your Special, ma'am!" Chuck opened the driver's side door and handed me a big, heavy cup. I had to let go of the paper to grab it.

"Oh wow, thanks." I pulled out the spoon that was sticking out of the hole on the plastic lid. It was covered with chocolate ice cream and a bunch of chunky stuff. "What is this?"

Fawn and Eric jumped into the back seat. I was being swarmed by adults.

"Double-fudge Brownie Blizzard with Oreos and Snickers. I invented it—the Samantha Special."

I took a big bite, which wasn't a good idea.

"Ice cream headache!" I pressed my fingers hard into my forehead, and then onto the sides of my nose. I can never tell exactly where that ice-cream-headache pain comes from.

"Drink this, quick!" Eric grabbed the Blizzard out of my hand and replaced it with a Styrofoam cup with a straw sticking out. I took a sip. Lots of syrup was in there. Not enough fizz. And I couldn't tell what brand of soft drink it was. So I took another sip. "What is this, a suicide?"

Eric shook his head. "Not quite. It is a mixture, but I only use caffeinated drinks."

"You know that I'm hardly ever allowed to drink this kind of stuff, right?" I looked back at Fawn, who was supposed to be my personal assistant or trainer or something like that. She thinks it's her job to keep me from eating and drinking unhealthy things. But instead of frowning like she normally does when I eat junk, she was smiling.

"Take another bite of your Special," she said.

Dad walked up to my side of the car and saw me push a huge spoonful of the Special into my mouth. "How do you like it?"

I couldn't say anything since the chunks and the ice cream filled every corner of my mouth. I held it all in there for a minute, letting it melt down my throat, since I didn't want to swallow so fast and get the ice cream headache again.

"Ya doin' better now, little lady?" Chuck shoved a big bite of something purple in his mouth and grinned.

I nodded. And then I felt it.

Chapter 6

It was kinda like a jolt. Or a buzz. Or a tingle. Well, whatever it was, it shot through my whole body. I'd experienced the feeling before, but not too many times. Once at a slumber party, after I ate two pieces of cake and three handfuls of red vines. Another time was at the fair when I ate a whole cotton candy and then finished off Brady's. Then there was that time at a campfire when I decided that the graham cracker and marshmallow wasn't necessary in a S'more, so I just ate the chocolate. Three bars of it.

I needed to run. Or I was going to explode.

"You know what? I really feel great! Can I get out of the car?" I sat the Special down on the seat and reached for the door handle.

"I knew it would work," Fawn said. "Peps me up every time."

The adults began to laugh and I pushed open the car door. The sugar was making my eyes twitch, and that was a lucky thing since they twitched right toward the paper that was sitting in the still-opened glove compartment. The sugar rush also made me extra brave for one split second, so I grabbed that paper and ran as fast as I could with it, away from the car and around to the back of the Dairy Queen.

I knew I would only have a minute to look at it before someone chased me down. I tried to focus on the paper, but for some reason, everything was blurry. I think it said "registration" at the top, but then I didn't know exactly where to look to find the state. I was huffing and puffing so hard from the running, and I think that sugar pulsing through my veins was making me kinda shaky. I kept turning my head, expecting to see one of the adults come stampeding around the corner and pounce on me. It would probably be Fawn first. *C'mon Riley. Calm down. And hurry up about it.*

I held my breath to stop the puffing. Still no adults. Whew.

I squinted down at the paper, and the word I was looking for finally became clear.

Chapter 7

Montana. Chuck's truck was registered in the state of Montana. Which meant we were in Montana, right?

The first and only adult to round the corner was Flip. That made no sense since he was the one with the ankle cast.

"I figured it out," I said, pointing to the registration. "We're in Montana."

Flip laughed, took a big bite of his ice cream, and took a long time swallowing it. "Looks like you win the crocheted bathtub."

"Huh? What's that supposed to mean?"

He laughed again. "Oh, it's something my granddad used to say at times like this."

"Times like what?"

"Times when I thought I'd outsmarted him, but I really didn't. You know, like winning a crocheted bathtub. It's not really a good prize, after all, since it won't hold water and—

"I don't get it."

Flip cleared his throat and sat down on the pavement. "Oh. Okay. Well, whatever. Anyway, we were going to tell you we're in Montana, Riley. Not sure why you had to get all weird about it."

"Weird? You think *I'm* getting weird? What about you? Until this week, I didn't even know who you *really* were."

Flip took another bite of his ice cream and took a long time to swallow again.

I sat down next to him. "By the way, I miss Flip."

"*Miss* him? I'm right here."

"Nah, you're some guy named Dan."

"What's the difference?"

"Flip made me laugh. Dan makes me nervous."

"So forget about him. You're calling me Flip anyway. It really is my nickname." He handed me a dripping spoonful of chunky stuff. "Want some?"

"What's in there? Doesn't look like Snickers or Oreos."

"This is the *Flip* Special. Vanilla ice cream with smashed-up French fries. Loads of caramel sauce."

I don't know why, but I took a bite. Now I knew why it took Flip a long time to swallow it. I was trying not to heave.

"Eww, what was that spicy thing?"

"Oh yeah, I forgot. I had them throw in a couple of jalapeños."

"That's gross."

"Yeah, well *your* ice cream is melting back in the car."
Flip stood up and offered me a hand. "Anything else I
can do to make your stay in Montana more pleasant?"

"I miss my friends and my mom. And my brother,
sort of. Can you fly them out here?"

Flip shook his head. "Jet's broke."

"But you have a backup, right?"

Flip nodded. "We'll have to see about that. But in the
meantime, I can introduce you to some new friends.
There are some nice kids about your age who live at our
secret cabin … uh, resort … place."

"Kids? Really? That sounds interesting."

"They *are* interesting."

Chapter 8

The interesting kids' names were Faith, Grace, Hope, and Sunday.

"Are you guys Christians?" I asked.

The oldest girl, Faith, answered. "Yes, our family loves Jesus. Grace, Sunday, and I were all baptized last year. Hope was not, because she is too little and does not understand. She thinks it is just swimming."

"I bath-tized my baby doll," Hope said. She held up a cute little doll with black skin.

"So," I asked, "have you always lived in Montana?" Judging from the clothing they were wearing, and the fact that they all talked with funny English accents, I suspected they were from somewhere else.

Sunday—the boy—answered. "Our home is in Kenya, Africa. We have lived here in Montana for only sixteen months. Mr. Flip brought us to the United States so I can receive medical treatments."

"Oh. That sounds good." I wanted to ask him what

kind of medical treatments, but I didn't want to be too nosy. Plus, all of a sudden I got distracted by the shoes Sunday was wearing.

"Are those Riley Mae shoes?" I pointed to the bright orange running shoes that were practically glowing on Sunday's feet.

The two younger sisters giggled. Grace spoke up. "We told him they are for girls. He does not care about that." Then they giggled louder, jumped up and down, and pointed at his feet.

That's when I noticed they were all wearing Riley Mae shoes. Each girl wore a different pair, and they looked really cute in them.

"Orange is my favorite color," Sunday said. "Why should girls get the shoes with all the best colors? Girls do not own the color orange."

Grace and Hope began chasing each other around in a circle, with Sunday in the middle. He put his hands to his mouth, and his eyes shifted from side-to-side.

"That is enough!" Big sister Faith grabbed both girls by the arms and led them back toward their house. Sunday looked relieved.

"Did you not bring any boys with you? I would like to play with someone who does not giggle so much."

"Umm, I do have a brother. He's eight. I hope he gets to come here to visit soon. How old are you?" Sunday seemed small, but smart, so I was stumped.

Chapter 8

"I am ten. And what about you, Miss Riley Mae?"

"Twelve."

"Same as Faith. She acts like she is my mother sometimes, because she is older. But I forgive her, because I think that God has made her bossy for a reason."

That made *me* giggle. "Ha! I think I'll tell my brother that one."

"Oh. Does that mean you are bossy too?"

I shrugged. "A little."

"I think that your brother and I will be good friends then."

Chapter 9

The next two weeks were really boring if you compare it to the week before, with the disaster on Half Dome, the finding out that bad guys are after us, the "sort of" plane crash, and the Dairy Queen meltdown. Pretty much, I got to hang out with my new friends and explore the huge, but somehow secret, Stevens resort. I wasn't allowed to go outside the gates, but who would want to? Inside was everything I needed, except my mom and brother. Well, I'm not sure I really needed my brother, but I was beginning to miss having him around. Some of the goofy stuff Sunday says reminds me of Brady, except Sunday always says things with this huge grin that makes it seem funny, unlike Brady, who smirks and just makes me mad.

"Mom and Brady will be here tomorrow," Dad said that night at our outdoor dinner "picnic." Fawn had packed ham sandwiches, potato salad, and watermelon in a basket and we all ate on a red-checked blanket by the lake.

"They're flying out on the backup jet," Flip said. Only it sounded more like "Her fyin ot duh hack uh jack," since he said it as he was shoving his face into a watermelon wedge. He chewed, swallowed, and wiped the mushy pink pulp on his sweatshirt sleeve. "They'll be here by noon, and we'll send Chuck to pick them up."

"Can I go?" I asked.

"No," everyone said.

"Ugh!" I slammed my fists on the blanket.

Dad looked surprised. "Riley! Do you really want to get back in Chuck's wild ride?"

He had a point.

Fawn pulled a chocolate cake out of a plastic carrier.

Grace and Hope squealed. "Mmmm! Cake!" Then they got up and ran in their famous circles, cheering, "Cake, cake, cake!" Their voices got higher and higher until they sounded like cars screeching to a halt over and over. I thought I was going to have to go tackle them and shove cake in their mouths to quiet them. Instead, their mother, Ajia, stood and said with a firm voice, "Cake comes to little girls who sit with good manners and do not squeal." Then she sat down and began cutting cake and serving it to us. She didn't offer any to them, since even though they had stopped squealing, they were still running. They kept looking over at us with frowns on their faces, like they were expecting us to bring them some cake.

"They will not get cake tonight," Faith said.

"Mother means what she says," Sunday added, and then he shoved a big piece of cake in his mouth.

Ajia sounds just like my mother.

"Have you ever been a police officer?" I asked Ajia.

Sunday laughed hard. "No, but she can run fast to catch the criminals!"

Ajia nodded. "It is true that I do not know about law enforcement. But I do train to run."

I noticed she was wearing a pair of running shoes. "So, you're an athlete?"

"Mother trained for the Olympics," Sunday said, "but could not run in the qualifying race because I got sick."

Ajia put her arm around Sunday. "It is fine, Son. You are more important to me than medals."

"Wait," I said, holding my hand up. "Are you talking about the real OLYMPICS? The every four years Olympics?"

"Yes," Ajia said. "I am a marathon runner."

"Her name—Ajia—means 'swift,'" Sunday said. "And she is!" His smile was full of chocolate cake.

Fawn put down her cake plate. "I need to stop eating this and go on a training run with you."

Ajia took a big bite of her cake and shook her head. "I am on hiatus, until God heals Sunday of his leukemia. All of my energy is for prayer and treatments right now. Running will come later, or it will not. I am at peace. God knows best."

Chapter 10

So that was it. Sunday had leukemia. I wished I had my computer with me so I could look it up. I knew it had something to do with blood cells not cooperating with your body and that you have to have treatments so you don't get too weak. I also knew that people die of leukemia sometimes, so it was amazing to me that none of Sunday's family seemed to be freaking out like I would be if I were them.

Sunday's Dad, Kiano, is the calmest of the whole family. He doesn't talk much—there's not much chance to talk with all those chatty girls he has—but he smiles a lot, even while he works hard around the Stevens' property. I watched him all week as he cleared brush and chopped wood. Smiling, smiling, smiling. And every time I passed by him, he would turn and say, "And how are you today, Miss Riley Mae? How is the shoe business?"

And I would smile back and answer, "I have no idea."

Then he would laugh and say, "Amen!"

I've never met someone so joyful in my whole life. I used to think that Bob Hansen, the head guy over at Swiftriver, was the most joyful person I ever met. But Bob acts more like he's practicing to be on a toothpaste commercial or something. Kiano's smile comes from his inside. Somewhere deep. I'd like to know where to get a smile like that.

Chapter 11

The backup jet was supposed to arrive at noon the next day. Chuck's SUV squealed into the driveway about eight minutes later.

"I'd write that cowboy a speeding ticket if I wasn't so glad to see all of you." Mom hugged everyone, leaving me for last. "How's my girl? I missed you so much!" She lifted my chin up and looked me right in the eyes, which almost started me crying again. "I brought you a surprise—"

"Surprise! I'm Huckleberry Hart!" It was Brady, running out from behind Chuck's SUV. He had something purple smeared all over his face.

"Tell me that's not my surprise," I said to Mom.

"Hey, you ought to be a little excited to see your brother. But no, that's not your surprise."

Mom walked to the other side of the SUV and opened the door.

A tall girl wearing "Teal and Steal" softball cleats jumped out.

It was Rusty!

Shari "Rusty" Peterson and I had become friends in the springtime, during softball season. It was after I had begged my parents to let me be the spokesgirl for the Riley Mae Shoe Collection. We signed a contract for two years, and then I found out that I wouldn't have any time to play softball, which is my favorite thing to do. I was pretty upset, and then I found out that Rusty was going to replace me as shortstop on the team. You would think that would lead us to be enemies and not friends. But it's hard not to like Rusty.

"Riley! Can you believe it? I get to stay for a week! I rode in a private jet! It was so cool! I've never even *been* in a plane before!"

Rusty looked good. Happier than when I last saw her and healthier. Rusty's naturally tall and slender, but she got a little too skinny when her Dad didn't have a job and they didn't have any food in the house. It was a secret we kept between the two of us for a while, and I was glad that her dad finally got a job at Swiftriver so I didn't have to sneak groceries to her anymore. Now if we could only find her mother . . .

"Montana is so pretty!" Rusty raised her hands up and twirled around. "Can you believe all these trees?"

"Wait. Who told you we were in Montana?"

"Your mom did when we landed. But she told me not to tell anyone because of the secret photo shoot and everything."

"Secret photo shoot?"

"Yeah, the one on the river. Riley, you are so lucky! I don't blame you for wanting to be a shoe model instead of playing softball. Oh, and my dad showed me the Ready Eddys. They're so cute! I'm gonna save up to buy some."

WHAT was this girl talking about? Secret photo shoot? Ready Eddys?

Dad ran up to greet Rusty with a high five, and then he put his arm around me. "So, what do you think about your surprise?"

"I-I ..." I couldn't comment. Too many surprises. And too much confusion.

Dad kneeled down and jokingly slapped my cheeks. Then he stood up and turned to Rusty. "Wow, she's speechless. That's a first. I guess we'll have to try to coax some words out of her over lunch."

"Lunch, yum!" Rusty looked all around. "Which direction is that?"

Dad pointed, and Rusty ran with her suitcase toward the house.

Dad jogged over to hug Mom, who was trying to wipe the purple off of Brady's face with a wet wipe. Then he shouted over to the rest of the group. "Anyone else hungry?"

"I'm starving!" A familiar voice trailed out from behind the SUV. It belonged to Matt Rainier, our trail guide from the Half Dome trip. He came over and shook my hand.

"So, Riley," Matt said, "I guess our adventures together aren't over. Your mom tells me that you've never been on a river rafting trip before. You're gonna love it!"

Flip hobbled over to greet Matt. "Hey, buddy, good to see you again!"

Matt tapped Flip's cast. "Yeah, and it's good to see you alive. You gave us all quite a scare, man. Don't *ever* fall off Half Dome again, okay?"

"Ha, I don't think Fawn will ever let me go near that trail again."

Matt got a funny little grin on his face. "How is Fawn? She had a pretty nasty scrape on her leg. Is she healing up okay?" He looked around like he was expecting someone to bring him a present or something.

"Let's go on in, and you can see for yourself." Flip tried to grab a suitcase from among a bunch Matt was carrying, but Matt fought back. "Don't think so. You concentrate on walking, and I'll lug this stuff."

We all piled inside the big lobby in the main lodge. Eric and Fawn were having a conversation on the cushy couch in front of the fireplace. When they saw us, they popped up, and Eric came over to greet us.

"You must be Matt," Eric said, and he shook Matt's

hand. "I'm Eric. My sister's been telling me a lot about you."

Fawn ran into the bathroom, which I thought was a weird thing to do. When she came out, her straight and shiny blonde hair was no longer in a ponytail, and it looked like she had applied some blush and lip gloss.

"Well, this is a surprise," she said.

Matt cleared his throat and put both his hands in the pockets of his jeans. He looked down at his shoes. "Good to see you again. How's the leg?"

"My leg? Oh that. I hardly notice it anymore. You did a good job fixing it up."

"I'm relieved to hear that. I hope I can keep you a little safer on the river."

"I'm glad you agreed to be our guide again."

Matt ran his fingers through his hair. "It's my pleasure."

Rusty jammed her elbow in my side, and I giggled because she hit me right in the ticklish part. "What did you do that for?"

Rusty whispered in my ear. "They like each other."

"Nuh-uh."

"Uh-huh. Keep watching. They're acting so weird."

I kept watching throughout lunch. Rusty was right, Matt and Fawn had a big old crush going on. Fawn kept complimenting Matt on his knowledge of the outdoors, and Matt told everyone about how tough Fawn had been when she scraped her leg during the Half Dome hike. One time they both grabbed for a roll and their hands touched. Fawn pulled hers back and then she turned all red.

"Would you like me to get you a roll?" Flip reached toward the basket. Flip smiled right at Matt and grabbed a roll, then buttered it for Fawn. "There you go. No need to be shy." Then he laughed and slammed his hand on the table, and most of our water glasses spilled over.

Mom interrupted the awkwardness. "Riley, why don't you take Rusty and Brady out and show them around?" She might as well have said, "Get out of here, kids. We adults have important stuff to talk about and we don't want you to hear it," because I'm pretty sure that's what she meant.

Dad emptied several cookies off a platter into a bag. "Take these and go have fun. It's nice outside right now."

And so we went. I wish we could have stayed to watch the new love birds in action, but I was also curious to hear if Mom had found the bad guys who tried to kill Flip on Half Dome.

Chapter 12

You have been eating huckleberries!" Sunday laughed and pointed to Brady's mouth. It was still purple despite Mom's wiping attempts.

"I love huckleberries!" Brady said. "But I'm all out. Do you know where I can get some more?"

"Oh yes. We can go for a hike and I will show you some bushes. But we must watch out for bears."

"Bears? Real bears?" Brady's eyes got huge.

"Oh yes. But mostly black bears. Grizzlies do not come around much."

"I want to see bears," Brady said.

"You have come to the right place. Would you like to go find some now?"

Brady looked at me like he wanted permission or something.

"Go ahead," I said. "Just don't get into any trouble. And make sure you listen to Sunday. He really knows his way around here."

"I will keep him safe," Sunday said. "Come on, friend. We will go look for Mary-Bear. She is the gentle one who comes down by the lake from time to time."

They both ran off. Brady yelled back. "Okay, I'm going with my friend Sunday!"

Hmm. I think that's the first time Brady's had a friend.

Chapter 13

Rusty and I decided to take a jog down to Chuck and Carmie's house to see some super-huge Dahlia flowers that Chuck told us about at lunch. We took off down the hill from the lodge, and it didn't take Rusty long to get ahead of me with those long legs of hers.

I pumped my arms a little harder and tried not to appear winded.

"So, how have you been, Rusty? I'm sorry I missed the softball tournament. The Half Dome hike was a little harder on me than I thought it would be." That was mostly true, but Rusty could never know the half of it. For now, she could only know that I was tired and sore and didn't make it out of bed in time to play.

Rusty slowed to a walk and pulled her long, reddish-brown hair to one side of her neck. "The first game was terrible. TJ was so mad that you weren't there, I think she lost her concentration and pitched a lousy game. Then, I let a ball go through my legs which scored the winning run for the other team. I didn't think she'd ever talk to me again."

"I'm so sorry. I wish I had been there."

"It's okay." Rusty smiled. "We ended up winning the tournament."

"No way."

"Yeah, I sorta got on a hitting streak. I pounded a walk-off home run in the next game, which got us back on track. You should see the trophy, it's huge."

I remembered back to some of those winning moments in softball. They were so fun. Would I ever get to do that again?

"So, TJ must have talked to you after *that*, right?"

"Yeah, she apologized for being mean. I think she's just so competitive that she loses track of what's important. I wish she had decided to come here with me."

"You mean she had a chance to come?"

"Yeah, your mom invited her, but she didn't want to miss the first game of All-Stars."

"Yep, that sounds like TJ. She'll never miss a game. But I wish she was here."

"Me too. But, hey, *I* came."

"And I'm glad you did."

I smiled and looked down at the Riley Mae Teal and Steal shoes that Rusty was wearing, and I remembered how cool it was that God helped me get those for her since her dad couldn't afford them. And that reminded me about a lesson I learned at church from Ephesians 6:15 in the Bible. It says, *"For shoes, put on the peace that comes from the Good News so that you will be fully prepared."* The verse isn't so much about real shoes, but more about sharing Jesus wherever we go. I'd been calling them the "Good News Shoes." I wondered if that was why Rusty was here in Montana—so I could share more about Jesus with her. I just wished I had a clue about how to do it.

We walked a little ways more and then stopped in front of Chuck and Carmie's cute little cottage. Rusty looked around. "So where are all the huge flowers?"

"I'm not sure. I would think they'd be right out here in the open."

We did see a couple of deer grazing in a bed of green stalks.

I scratched my head. "I wonder—"

"Hi there!" Hope poked me in the back, which made me jump. "Do you want to play hide-and-seek with us?"

I turned and was surprised to see all three sisters. How had they snuck up on me? You'd think I would have heard a giggle or something.

"NO way," I said, and then I turned to Rusty. "I've been trying to find them for two weeks. They have *way* too many hiding places!"

"But we want to play with you guys," Hope whined.

"That's fine with me," Rusty said. "What can we do instead of hide-and-seek?"

"We can go scare the boys," Grace said.

Faith frowned. "Mother would not like that."

"But they will not tell Mother because they will be too embarrassed to tell her they were scared by girls."

"That is true," Faith said. "But it would not be nice."

"But it would be fun," Hope smiled.

I liked these adventurous little girls.

"Let's go find the boys," I said.

We spent what seemed like a half-an-hour looking for Brady and Sunday, and we almost gave up until we spied them hiding behind a big storage box a few feet from the boat house. They kept poking their heads out and pointing toward the trees which lined the other side of the lake.

"They are looking for Mary-Bear," Faith said. "She sometimes comes down to that side of the lake in the late afternoon to eat berries from the huckleberry bushes."

"Should we be leaving then?" Rusty looked worried.

"Oh no. Mary is not dangerous. She minds her own business, as long as we stay out of her way. The one we need to watch out for is Herod-Bear."

"Herod?" Rusty said. "That's a funny name for a bear."

"He is crazy," Hope said as she made googly eyes.

Faith explained. "We named him Herod because he is the meanest person we could think of from the Bible. The rangers have been trying to capture Herod and take him far into the woods so he does not hurt anyone. So far, he has only clawed at some of our buildings."

"And he broke my favorite canoe right in half," Grace said with a frown.

I suddenly wanted to go inside where there were no bears.

"Herod has not been around for a long time," Faith said.

That didn't change my mind.

"Hey, would you girls like to go play in the game room with us?" I asked.

"Yes!" They all ran up toward the lodge.

"They have a game room too? This place is crazy nice," Rusty said.

"Yeah. We can play pool, ping-pong, board games, darts. And there's a hot chocolate machine!"

"So we better get in there quick." Rusty took off running. Of course, she beat me up the hill.

I guess the boys weren't going to get scared ... today.

Chapter 14

That night, Mom called me and the grown-ups into the living room for a "briefing." That's where they let you in on important stuff you need to know—only they usually don't tell you the really scary stuff.

"How come Rusty knows everything, and I know nothing?" I asked.

"What are you talking about? We haven't told Rusty a thing. She only knows that we're all here so we can do a secret photo shoot on the river. We had to tell her that much so we could get her to come. Aren't you happy about that?" Mom had her arms crossed and her right eyebrow raised.

How does she do that? I tried to raise one eyebrow, then the other. It didn't work for me.

"Riley," Dad said, "are you going to answer your mom?"

"Oh, sorry. Yeah, I'm happy Rusty's here. What are Ready Eddys?"

"River sandals," Fawn said. "The newest shoes in the Riley Mae Sport Collection. Wait till you see them. They're turquoise with chunks of gold."

"Real gold? What do they cost—a thousand dollars now?" I still wasn't too happy with the price of Riley Mae shoes. If I didn't get them for free, I wouldn't be able to afford my own shoes.

"No—it's like the fool's gold you see in the rivers," Matt said.

I wondered why Matt was in this briefing. Did he know everything about Flip and Fawn and Swiftriver now?

"So, why did you name a shoe after a guy named Eddie?" I asked Dad. My dad owns his own advertising business, and Swiftriver hired him to help with the marketing of the Riley Mae collection. He's been the one naming all the shoes.

Matt, the outdoor expert, filled me in. "They're not named after a guy named Eddie. An eddy is a water current you find on a river. Anytime you see an obstruction, like a rock or a tree limb, on the other side, you'll find a swirling current that goes the opposite direction of the rest of the water."

"Like a whirlpool?" I asked.

"Yes," Matt said. "That's exactly what it is. You also find them on every bend in a river. Sometimes an eddy will suck you in, which is bad if you want to keep going. Other times, it can be good."

"Like when you don't want to be swept downriver and over a twenty foot waterfall," Flip added.

Fawn held her hand up. "Let's change the subject, please."

"Yes, let's do," Mom said. "I need to bring you all up to date on our investigation into Flip's accident." Mom looked over at Flip and Fawn. "The good news is, we've checked on all the people on your long list of suspects. They're minding their own business these days. None of them have been anywhere near California, and we've had several detectives tracking them to see if they have any unusual contacts with anyone in the Fresno area. Nothing's turned up."

Matt was still in the room, so I figured he must know about some of the secrets. "So," he said, "can we assume that Flip's accident was just that—an accident?"

"Maybe," Mom said. "It could be that someone really was collecting rocks on top of Half Dome for souvenirs, and then they lost their grip on the backpack at a bad time."

"But why wouldn't they stop to see if he was okay?" Fawn was getting that horrified look again.

Matt put his hand on her shoulder. "Well, you aren't allowed to collect things and take them out of national parks. Maybe it was a kid or someone who thought they would be in big trouble if someone found out, especially since the rocks almost killed someone."

Fawn shivered. "I don't know. That sounds too coincidental to me. Plus, what about all those other times when we thought we were being watched or followed?"

Mom chuckled. "Well, let's see. The suspicious reporter in Arizona turned out to be Eric."

Yikes. How did my mom find out about that?

"The guy with the runaway dog at Fawn's house was Eric. Then there was the prowler in front of our house . . ."

"The Easter Sneaker!" I jumped up and pointed at Eric.

Flip threw two balled-up socks at his brother. I'm not sure where he got those, since he never wears socks.

"Sorry, bro!" Eric said as he caught the socks. "I really wanted to find you guys."

"You could have called." Fawn pointed to her phone. "Or texted."

"Very funny. Like I had your number."

"Well, once you were sure it was us, you could have rung the doorbell."

Eric crossed his arms. "I didn't know if I was being followed or if someone was watching you. It would be pretty bad if your own brother blew your cover, wouldn't it?"

"So, where do we go from here?" Dad asked.

"Well," Mom said, "Tyler's mechanic is still checking into that plane malfunction, but I'd say if nothing more turns up, we all go back to Fresno."

Fawn's smile returned. "And we can continue to run Swiftriver?"

"I don't see why not," Mom said. "Now that we know who you all really are, we can keep a more careful eye on things."

"I'm sorry we didn't tell you in the first place," Fawn said. "I really thought we were safe with our new identities. You must think we're terrible to get your family caught up in this mess." Fawn hid her face in her hands.

"It doesn't look like there is much of a mess anymore," Dad said. "And hey—we got a pretty nice vacation out of it." He turned to Mom. "Just let me have another week of fishing . . . please?" He clasped his hands together and grinned.

"What about the photo shoot?" Flip asked. "When are we going to do that?"

"Yeah," Eric said, "I don't want you guys going back to California so soon." Then he threw the socks back in Flip's direction. "I've missed you."

"I'm going out tomorrow to check on the middle fork of the river," Matt said. "I think this time of year it ought to have some good rapids going. I need to find some that aren't too difficult to navigate, but that will look treacherous for the photos. I'd say if everything goes according to plan, I could get you all trained up, and we could run the river by the end of the week."

"Trained up? What do we have to train for?" I remembered back to the torture training Fawn put me through on the Stairmaster when we were getting ready for the Half Dome hike.

"It won't be too hard, Riley," Matt said. "I'll need to take you out on some Class Two and Class Three rapids so you can get used to paddling according to my commands. Then you can run the Class Fours more confidently."

All those classes made me nervous. "Wait—I'm not doing this by myself, right?"

"Nope," Fawn said. "This photo shoot's going to be all girls this time. Me, you, your mom, and if her dad says okay, Rusty too. We're all going to be wearing Ready Eddys."

"Uh, you have to have one man with you." Matt kicked the side of Fawn's shoe. "But I'll pull my hair back in a ponytail if you want."

Fawn blushed. "Oh yeah, we need our guide. But we're going to cut him out of the advertising photos. The theme for this ad is "Riley Mae Girl Day—This Is Not a Tea Party.""

"I like it," I said.

"Okay then," Mom said, "consider yourselves briefed. I'll let you know if I find out anything else."

As we all got up to leave, Mom reminded us of one more thing:

"Don't forget that we still have Rusty here, so we can't

disclose any details of the Half Dome accident. For now, she just knows that Flip fell and broke his ankle."

That was going to be tough. Before my association with Swiftriver, I didn't have to keep secrets from anybody. I could say whatever was on my mind. Now I had to think before I opened my mouth, or better yet, press some of that pink sparkly duct tape over my lips.

Luckily, when I found Rusty in our room, she didn't ask why she hadn't been invited to the "briefing." She had been on the phone talking to her dad the whole time.

"How is your dad?" I asked.

"He's doing great. He loves his job at Swiftriver. I think maybe he was depressed when he didn't have a job for all that time. And it's been so hard to take care of me without my mom around to help."

Rusty's mom left her family when Rusty was around five years old. That's all I knew. That, and Rusty showed me a letter once from her mom to her dad saying she had to leave because they had a child. The whole thing makes no sense to me because Rusty's about the sweetest girl I know. I'd been praying that someday, somehow, Rusty would find her mom. Until then, I was glad her dad was at least doing better.

"Oh!" Rusty grabbed her suitcase and hoisted it up on the bed. "I almost forgot! Sean sent you something."

Sean is this cute boy at church who likes me. And I like everything about him except his last name—

O'Reilly. He's been asking me to marry him since we were in kindergarten. But it's never going to happen, since I can't imagine having the name Riley O'Reilly.

Rusty pulled a white box with a pink bow out of her suitcase. It had a big tag on it that said: "I miss you! Come back!"

"Sean has nice penmanship," Rusty smiled and elbowed me in the ribs.

Inside the box were two chocolate donuts and a card that said, "Every week, Love, Sean."

Sean saves a chocolate donut for me every week at church. Apparently, he didn't intend to stop.

"I think Sean's adorable," Rusty said, as she took a bite of one of the donuts without even asking for my permission. I grabbed the other one and chomped. We both frowned a little.

"A bit stale," I said, "but you can't waste anything chocolate."

"Yeah." Rusty brushed some crumbs off her lips. "Got any milk to wash this down?"

We headed to the kitchen, where we found some better chocolate, in the form of brownies. It didn't take us long to finish off the pan, but then we had to stay up past midnight waiting for the sugar buzz to wear off.

Chapter 15

"Riley, Rileeeeey!" A talking purple bear with bad breath was shaking me and calling my name. "I wanna go fishing."

I opened my eyes and found out it was Brady.

"Ewww, get away. You smell really bad right now."

"But I want to go fishing, and Sunday said we have to go early."

I sat up and looked out the window of the room where Rusty and I were sleeping. Dark. I flopped back down and covered my head with my blankets.

"Go away. It's night."

"No, it's not. It's five o'clock. I told Sunday I'd be at the lake at five thirty to fish."

"Then go."

"I can't go by myself."

"Ugh! Then don't go." I turned over on my stomach and put my head under my pillow.

"But I want to go too." That was a different voice. Rusty. She was up out of bed with her jacket on already.

I sat up and stared at her through the wavy mop of hair that covered my eyes. "Are you kidding? You want to go out there in the dark and catch stinky fish?"

"Aw, come on, Riley. We have our own lake and everything. Why not?"

"Yeah, listen to your friend," Brady said.

It was clear I wasn't getting out of this. I waved my finger at Brady. "*You* have to go tell Mom and Dad where we're going. I'm not waking them up and making them mad."

"I wrote them a note, and I left it in the bathroom."

"Okay, then. Let's get this over with." I heaved myself out of bed and put on some jeans and a hooded sweatshirt. I didn't know what shoes I was supposed to wear for mucking around on the shore of a lake.

"What are those big plastic boots called that come up to your waist? I need Swiftriver to make me some of those." I moaned and grabbed a pair of flip-flops.

"Hurry up, Riley." Brady was hanging on the doorknob. "Sunday's gonna think I forgot to come."

"It would have been nice," I said, as I grabbed a flashlight, "if you had told me about this silly plan last night!" I stomped out of the room. Rusty giggled and followed.

We trekked down the hill from the lodge to the lake. It was a good thing I brought the flashlight. Since there were no city lights and no moon, the place was pitch-black. One small light shone in the distance. It was attached to Sunday's head.

"You brought the girls! That is wonderful. We will load up the bigger boat."

"We're going out in a boat? Cool!" Rusty was obviously more adventurous than me at this time of the morning.

"Wait," I said. "We can't go out in the dark, can we?"

Sunday laughed. "Miss Riley Mae, do you not have boating shoes?" He pointed to my old flip-flops. I noticed he was wearing the same flaming-orange Riley Mae running shoes.

"Well, you should talk. Look what you're wearing."

"This is all I wear," Sunday said. "I own seven pairs. Remember? I like orange."

"Well, I hope they don't scare the fish away," I said. But on second thought, I sorta hoped they would, since I didn't want to be dealing with any slimy old fish.

"Are we taking the motorboat?" Brady asked.

"No, too noisy," Sunday said. "We can row this one." Sunday grabbed some fishing gear from a big equipment box and arranged it neatly inside a midsized rowboat. "Girls, you get in, and Brady and I will push us out. Mmm ... I can smell fish this morning."

The boys got soaking wet during the push-in maneuver, but they didn't seem to mind. Brady had an ear-to-ear grin after he hopped in. He seemed a little more grown up to me here in Montana.

"We do not have to row out far, the lake gets deep fast," Sunday said.

"How do you know there are fish in here?" I asked.

"Mr. Chuck had them stock some lake trout last week. I watched the helicopter dump some huge ones in."

So that's where the fish come from that are in lakes. But, I wondered, where do they get them in the first place?

Sunday helped Brady prepare a fishing line with a nasty worm. The poor thing squirmed all over, and then when it was hooked, it bled all over.

"Yuck," I said.

"You just row and let us men catch the fish," Brady said.

Rowing is a little hard to do when you're still half-asleep. "Rusty, can you grab an oar and help me?" We both sat in the middle of the boat and made a mean rowing team.

"Okay!" Sunday said. "You can stop now. You got us out quick."

"Good, now I can sleep," I said, and I lay down across the middle seat of the boat and closed my eyes. But something kept me from falling asleep. Cold.

So I sat up and asked Sunday if there was an extra fishing pole and if he had any kind of bait I could use that wouldn't bleed all over me. He handed me a ball of cheese. I sniffed it. "This smells nasty."

"It is not for you to eat," Sunday said.

Then he laughed his special Sunday laugh. I think it starts from his toes somewhere and gains momentum until it pops out of his mouth and makes me jump every time. Then I can't help laughing too.

"Put it on the hook," Sunday said. "Fish sometimes go for it."

After I jammed it on, Sunday showed me how to cast the line out into the lake. Funny, as much as my dad loves fishing, we'd never done it together, and no one else had ever taught me. I kinda liked casting and then reeling in the line. So I practiced over and over.

Sunday grabbed my right hand to stop me from reeling. "You must leave it alone for a while or the fish will never see the bait."

"So, I'm just supposed to sit here and wait?"

"Yes. You must be patient."

No wonder Dad never took me fishing before.

Brady, on the other hand, was frozen like a statue at the front of the boat. The only thing moving on him was his eyes—back and forth, scanning the water.

Ha. Like he could see anything in the dark.

"Ooh! I think I caught something!" Rusty bounced up and down on the seat and pulled back her fishing pole.

Sunday yelped. "It is me. You have hooked my pants."

Sunday pulled a hook from the bottom of his right pant leg. "I am glad you missed my leg."

Rusty put her hand to her mouth. "Oh no! I'm so sor—"

"GADZOOKS! I've got him! He's big and I've got him!" Brady emerged from his statue-coma by jumping up and down in the boat while he reeled like a madman.

Brady's jumping caused the boat to dip back and forth. I slipped right off where I was sitting on the middle seat onto the wet floor of the boat.

"Brady, knock it off! You're gonna flip us!"

Sunday moved over next to Brady to help coach him.

"Oh yes, you certainly do have a big fish! Do not pull too hard. Reel a bit, then rest, and let him take the line. Now, pull again. He will get tired."

Sunday reached a hand back in my direction. "Riley, please give me the net."

Behind me in the back of the boat was a pile of fishing junk. And at the bottom of the junk was the net. I held it out to Sunday. "You're not going to put the fish in that, are you?"

"Unless you would like to hold it in your lap until we get to shore," Sunday said. Then he laughed again.

"I'm getting tired." Brady shook his reeling hand. "My fingers are numb."

"Come on, Brady," Rusty said. "You can do it. Don't give up. I wanna see how big that fish is." I guess that bit of encouragement should have come from me, but I didn't think of it.

Brady mustered some new strength and began reeling and pulling again. We all watched in amazement as my brother continued the battle for what seemed like at least ten more minutes. Then something splashed next to the boat.

Sunday had jumped in. Or had he fallen in? I was about to panic when Sunday's head popped up above the surface.

"He is enormous!" Sunday yelled.

He was holding the net in the water, and in the net was a big, ugly fish. Well, most of the fish was in the net. The back of the fish hung out at least a foot.

"What should we do?" Rusty held a life vest in one hand, an oar in the other, *and* she pinched her fishing pole between her knees.

"Row us in! This monster cannot come in the boat. He will flip out." Sunday hugged the netted fish close to his body. "Brady, keep a tight hold on your pole, but do not reel anymore."

Brady stiffened back to statue position and smiled. "I knew I had a big one."

Rusty and I returned to our rowing job in the middle of the boat, and in no time we made it to shore. Sunday and the monster fish swam alongside the whole way,

and as soon as we got to shallow water, Brady jumped in
to help Sunday drag up his catch.

"He weighs a ton! I can't wait to show Dad!"

Rusty and I waited until the boat reached the beach
before we jumped out. No sense getting all wet just
to see a slimy sea creature. Plus, I didn't want to be
involved at all with getting it off the hook.

Sunday had him off the hook by the time we got
there. He pulled a knife out of his pants pockets.

"What're you gonna do with that?" I asked.

"The most humane thing." He raised the knife up, the
point directed at the fish's head. I closed my eyes …

And then I heard huffing and snorting.

Chapter 16

"What was that?" Rusty asked.

I opened my eyes and looked around. It was still pretty dark, so I could only see shadows.

Sunday dropped the knife and pointed his headlamp into the trees behind us.

"Uh-oh," he said.

The huffing and snorting sounds got closer and then snapping too.

Brady's mouth dropped open. "Is th-that Mary-Bear?"

"Yes, it could be," Sunday said.

"So, we should take the fish and get out of here," Brady said.

We all jumped back as a bear shape emerged from the trees.

"No, the fish stays," Sunday said. "Follow me!"

We all ran toward the big equipment box where all the boating and fishing supplies had been stored.

I ditched my flip-flops, sprinted in my bare feet and reached the box in a matter of seconds.

"Hurry!" Sunday climbed a little stepladder and swung the big lid open and reached out his hand. "Come on! Get in here!"

I looked back in horror to see the bear moving toward us. Brady seemed to be taking his time behind me.

"Brady! Hurry!"

"I want my fish!"

"Who cares about that stupid fish? Get in the box!"

I ran back, grabbed my brother by the arm, and dragged him up the stepladder. I had to give him an extra little boost to get him over the side of the box.

"Oww! You threw me into something hard!"

Sunday shined his light in and pointed to the far corner of the box.

"Girls, you jump over there, into that pile of life vests."

Rusty and I jumped in, and Sunday followed. The walls of the box stood about two feet over our heads. Now we had to figure out how to get the big lid closed.

The huffing got closer.

"Do you think she'll leave us alone in here?" I asked.

"If it is Mary, she will. But if it is Herod—"

Sunday was interrupted by a loud growl and a smashing sound. I grabbed his light and shined it out of one of the cracks of the box, just in time to see Herod crushing a metal trash can to smithereens.

"We have to get this lid closed," Rusty said. "I saw a rope down there next to the stepladder." She lifted her foot up. "Here, give me a lift."

"You can't go out there!" I said.

"I'm tall and I'm fast. Give me a lift. Hurry!"

"Ah no! He's eating my fish." Brady had Sunday's headlamp now, and he was watching out the crack as Herod ripped up the lake trout.

Sunday looked out the crack. "Perfect. He is distracted. It is now or never."

We lifted Rusty up and out of the box. I heard a thump and then a moan.

"Rusty, are you all right?"

"Yeah. Just scraped my arm on something."

"Please hurry," I cried.

In seconds, Rusty's head popped up over the wall of the box. She held up the end of a rope. "Got it. I think I can tie it on the ring on this lid."

It seemed like forever before she dragged herself back over the side of the box.

"Good thing I know knots," she said as she jumped back in, carrying the other end of the rope with her. As she pulled the rope, the lid rose up, and then it came down and slammed a couple of feet above us, blocking all light except what was coming from Sunday's headlamp and the crack.

"Uh-oh," Brady said. "Here he comes!"

Herod was on his way to the box. I didn't even have to look out the crack to know that, because the snorting and growling got closer until it was right next to us.

"Everyone help me hold this rope. We've got to keep the lid down!" Rusty grabbed our hands and placed them on the rope, since we couldn't see. "Lean all your weight into it!"

Herod smacked the side of the box, and we all screamed. No way this old wood was going to hold up to that strength. We heard metal crunching near the front of the box. Poor stepladder never had a chance. Then ... heavy thumping above our heads.

"He's trying to smash the box in!" Brady yelled.

"Shhh ... and keep holding the rope," Rusty whispered.

More thumping and snorting. A board broke up above us, and I saw something come through. Brady shined the light up on a large, black paw.

Sunday grabbed the light and turned it off.

"Keep holding," Rusty said.

That's when we felt it. Tension from the other side of the rope. Herod wasn't smacking down anymore. He was pushing up on the end of the box lid.

"We can't win a tug-of-war against a bear!" I yelled. Even so, I pulled harder.

"Lord, we need your help," Sunday said. "Give us your strength right now."

"Yeah, Lord, what he just said," Rusty added.

I stayed silent as the rope tore harder at my hands, and I tried to hold on.

But Brady let go. "I have an idea," he said, and he moved to the back of the box and started pounding on the side of it.

I couldn't believe it. "Brady, you knucklehead! Get back here!"

"I'm going to try to distract him. Sunday, pound on the other side of the box."

Sunday shrugged, kept one hand on the rope, and pounded on the other side of the box.

The tugging stopped. The huffing and snorting stopped too. All we heard was a dragging noise, as the bear circled the box for a while.

"He's walking around us," Brady whispered. "Let's be real quiet. Maybe we made him hungry." Brady grinned, and looked out the crack.

Sure enough, Herod had grown tired of fighting for the kid meal-in-the-box and decided to go finish his fish breakfast on the beach.

We all took turns watching out the crack in the box. The fish was big, and Herod took his time eating it, bones and all. Then he lay down on the beach.

"Oh, great," I said. "He's taking a nap. What're we supposed to do now?"

"Stay here," Sunday said. "We cannot leave until we

are sure he is gone. It should not be long." Sunday's voice sounded a little shaky.

"Are you okay" I asked.

"Yes, but I am a little cold," he said. That's when I remembered that Sunday was wet from swimming with the fish in the lake.

"Here, wear my sweatshirt." At first Sunday refused, but I forced him to take it. "You have to keep warm. Who knows how long we're gonna be in this box."

Herod stayed resting on the beach for a long time. Then he got up and walked around, sniffing at things along the shore. Once in a while, he smacked at something on the beach and huffed a few times. Thankfully, he never turned his attention back to our box, but we couldn't take the chance he might see us if we tried to get out. So we stayed put. The sun finally came out all the way. We could tell by the light coming in the crack and in the hole Herod had made on top of the box.

The few rays of light shining in made it seem warmer, even if it wasn't, and it felt nice to finally see everyone and our surroundings. Not that the surroundings were very exciting. Just a bunch of life vests, more fishing nets, and some broken oars. I held up one of the oars. "I guess this is what you fell into, Brady."

"Yeah, but I'm okay."

I noticed Rusty examining something on the inside of her right forearm.

"What is that?" I asked.

"Torn skin," she said. "I caught my arm on something as I was jumping over the wall to get the rope."

I shivered as I inspected the deep, jagged cut on Rusty's arm. Dried blood had stained the inside of her hand and the in-betweens of her fingers, and new blood was still slowly escaping from the wound.

"That is going to need some stitching," Sunday said. He reached over and patted Rusty on the shoulder with his shaky hand. "You were very brave to go out and get that rope."

"Well, I don't think it was bravery. It's hard to explain, but all of a sudden I knew I had to get out there and get that rope, and so my body started moving. If I had taken a minute to think, I probably wouldn't have done it."

"And we would have been Herod's breakfast," Brady said.

At the mention of breakfast, my stomach rumbled.

Sunday laughed. "Do you wish you had some of that cheese bait, Riley Mae?"

"No, but I bet you wish you had some dry clothes on."

Sunday's teeth chattered and then he coughed. And that cough didn't sound very good to me.

Chapter 17

We stayed in the box a long time. Herod had moved out of our limited field of vision from the box crack, but from time to time we still heard snapping and what we thought was some kind of animal movement from outside. Since the day was now in full force, it could have been ducks or squirrels for all we knew, but the scare from Herod early that morning had put a fear in us that made us stay put. Anyway, I figured our parents would be out to get us in no time, as soon as they saw the note from Brady.

"So, in the note, you *did* say we were fishing at the lake, right?" I had to ask, because sometimes my brother likes to leave cryptic notes that no one can figure out.

"Yes, I gave them all the details. I wrote that we went to the lake at five o'clock, and we were fishing with Sunday."

"Well, that's good," I said. "They should be here to look for us any minute now, since we didn't show up for breakfast."

"Yeah, as soon as Dad shaves."

Now that was the kind of comment that can only mean trouble when it comes from my brother.

"What do you mean by that?" I glared down my nose at him.

"By what?" He didn't look at me back.

"Why does Dad have to shave?"

Brady crossed his arms in a huff. "So he can see the note, of course."

"What ... did you put the note in the shaving cream?"

"NO, I did *not* put it in the shaving cream. That would be impossible."

"Well, that's a relief."

"The note is on the mirror," Brady said. "But Dad needs some steam from shaving to see it. You know how he and Mom leave those love notes for each other on the mirror? It's science. Anyone can leave a regular note."

I glanced at Sunday, who was still shivering but half-asleep, and I watched Rusty, who was grimacing while pressing one of her socks into her wound to soak up the bleeding. And then I yelled at my brother.

"Yes, any *regular* person would leave a *regular* note! Ugh! Haven't you noticed that Dad hasn't shaved in days? He thinks he's a mountain man now. C'mon Brady!

I thought you were supposed to be smarter than me!" I
kicked an oar in his direction.

Brady slumped in the corner. "I'm sorry! I thought
it would be a fun way to leave a note. I didn't know all
this would happen with the fish and the bear." Then he
started crying. "And I don't want Sunday to die ..."

Sunday woke from his half nap. "What did you say,
my friend?"

"I don't want you to die. From leukemia. And getting
too cold. It would be my fault."

"That is not going to happen," Sunday said. "Anyway,
if I died, I would end up in heaven, which is much better
than here. So then I would thank you, if it had been your
fault, but it would not have been."

"Huh?" Brady scratched his head.

"He's not making sense," Rusty said. "Maybe if we put
some of these life vests on top of him it will warm him
up some more."

"I am making good sense. Heaven is our true home.
It is beautiful and there is no sadness, pain, or sickness.
God is there too. I am excited to go someday. But not
today because of a mad bear. Anyway, Brady, you were
the one who distracted Herod away from us."

"I sometimes wonder if my mom is in heaven." Rusty
tipped her head back to look out the hole on the lid
of the box. Tears filled up in her eyes, and when she

blinked, one slid down her cheek and ran down her arm and into the cut.

My whole body warmed up all at once. "No, she's not," I said.

"How do you know?" she asked.

"I'm not sure, but it's probably like how you just knew you were supposed to climb out of the box to get that rope. Don't worry, I'm sure you're going to find your mom real soon."

A little more time passed, and life in the box actually got stuffy from the sun beating down. Then we finally heard it—the call of the "Mountain Man."

"Rileeeeeey! Bradyyyyyy!" I spied Dad out of the crack of the box. He was running, calling out toward the lake. His facial hair was gone.

"Hey, Brady," I smiled at my brother. "Your note worked."

Chapter 18

I didn't think I'd be anywhere near a hospital again so soon after the Half Dome disaster, but here I was in the emergency room at Kalispell Regional Hospital, waiting for Sunday and Rusty to be checked out. Rusty's problem was obvious—her arm looked like raw hamburger. Sunday's problem was a little more complicated.

"If his immunities are lowered, it could affect his leukemia treatment." Sunday's mom looked calm, but concerned. "He will need to stay overnight so they can do tests."

"I knew it," Brady said. "Can I go see him?"

"Not yet, but soon you can when he is in his own room. He asked that you go back to the house and pick up a pair of dry, orange shoes. Will you do that?" Sunday's mom ruffled Brady's hair with her hand. "By the way, Sunday said that you caught the biggest fish he has ever seen."

"It's too bad the bear ate it," Brady said. "Dad, can we go get the shoes now?"

My dad stroked his clean-shaven chin. "Sure. Mom can stay here with the girls. Maybe we can also pick out a fishing magazine for you and Sunday to look at together."

"Yeah," Brady said.

My mom, Rusty, and I remained behind for the "hamburger" treatment.

A nurse named Diane made a nasty face when she first saw Rusty's arm.

"Wow, that's a mess. Do you know what you caught it on?" She took a brown bottle of something out of a cabinet and popped the cap. "This is going to sting."

"Well," Rusty said, "I'm not exactly ... ouch ... sure, because it was dark ... ooh, that does sting ... but I'm pretty sure it was a nail or a piece of jagged wood. Whew. Are you done torturing me yet?"

"Not until we get all the debris out of your arm. Looks like it was wood, because there are lots of pieces of something in here." Diane turned to my mom. "When did your daughter have her last tetanus shot?"

Mom looked confused. "Oh, this isn't my daughter. She's my daughter's friend." She put her hand on Rusty's shoulder. "We didn't do a very good job taking care of you, did we Rusty?"

Diane stopped her torture treatment. "Oh, I see." She

grabbed a clipboard and flipped through some paperwork. "We contacted your parents, right? For permission
to treat?"

"Oh, I'm sure they did," Mom said. "We just got off the
phone with her dad."

Diane flipped through the papers some more. "Hang
on," she said, and she disappeared out the door.

"I bet you're glad she's gone," I said. "You want me to
hide that brown bottle?"

Rusty managed a ragged smile. "Please."

A few minutes later, a different nurse appeared. "I'm
Erma. I'll be finishing up your treatment here and then
the doctor will see you. Nurse Diane was pulled away to
treat another patient, but she told me that you still had
some chunks in your arm I need to fish out."

Erma looked at Rusty's arm and winced. "My, that is
a nasty wound." She grabbed a sponge out of a jar and
took a minute to look around on the counter. Then she
turned toward us, hands on her hips. "Have you girls
seen a brown bottle anywhere around here?"

Chapter 19

It turned out that Rusty only needed five stitches. The doctor pulled the rest of the hamburger together with butterfly bandages. She did have to get a tetanus shot, which Rusty said hurt more than the initial scrape and the brown bottle solution combined.

"She can't get her arm wet for a week," the doctor said. That meant Rusty wouldn't be going on the river-rafting photo shoot.

"Can't we postpone it?" I used my best whiny voice during a private meeting that night after Rusty had gone to bed, but it did no good.

"Sorry, Honey," Dad said. "Matt only has two weeks off, so we need to get the practice runs in, and then the shoot needs to happen right after that. We also need to leave some time in case the weather doesn't cooperate."

"Actually, we all have jobs we need to get back to," Mom said.

"Maybe we should hire you on at Swiftriver so you could be our personal bodyguard," Flip said.

"I'll take that job," Matt said, and he smiled at Fawn.

Fawn didn't look like she would mind that one bit.

"My hope," Mom said, "is that you won't need a bodyguard. Our investigation hasn't turned up anything."

That's what I wanted to hear. If we didn't have any bad guys to hide out from, our lives could get back to normal again. Of course, I still had this shoe contract to do, and that had jolted me out of anything normal.

Mom continued. "Rusty's dad did say that she could stay here for an extra week, as long as her arm is healing properly. Since he has to work every day, he would rather have her here with us instead of at home with nothing to do."

I almost forgot that Rusty lives with her dad in an old apartment building in a rough part of town. That was her "normal." I never really thought about what she did when he was at work. My parents are able to adjust their work schedules so one of them is always home with me and my brother. It's not like I need someone to watch me every second, but I'm not sure about Brady. He's always going to science camp where he learns how to do these risky experiments, but then he wants to try them at home. He's smart, but kinda clumsy, so I'm pretty sure he could blow the house up if he wasn't supervised.

"Rusty ripped her arm up pretty good," Matt said. "Anyone hear how Sunday's doing?"

"Well," Dad said, "I didn't say this when Brady was around, but they are a little concerned about his red blood count. It's dropped a little too much—"

Flip kicked a chair with his good foot. "That poor kid! He's already had one bone marrow transplant, and I don't know what they're going to do if he ends up needing another one."

"Then, let's pray that he won't," Matt said. Then he grabbed Fawn's hand and held it. She looked up at him with adoring eyes, and he looked back and grinned. When Matt also grabbed Flip's hand, we finally figured out that Matt wanted to pray *right now*, so we all joined hands.

"Dear God, we ask that you would please heal Sunday. He and his family have been through a lot of difficulties, and we would love to see the leukemia gone and his family able to return home and be normal again. We ask this in Jesus' name, Amen."

"Normal" was starting to confuse me. For Sunday, getting back to normal would be good. For Rusty, not so good. For me ... well, I had a feeling that I wouldn't have to worry too much about that, because it was never going to happen.

Chapter 20

We all went to the hospital the next day to get Sunday out of there. The doctor told his family that it was okay for him to go home just as long as they made an appointment at the Missoula Cancer Center for the next week.

For fun, we put together an "orange parade." Each of us brought an orange gift, and we presented it to Sunday as he exited the hospital doors in his wheelchair. Brady gave him an orange helium balloon, and I gave him some orange tulips that I got from Carmie. Rusty brought a bag of baby carrots, and Fawn gave him a box of those yummy little tangerines. Sunday's mom brought him a new pair of orange sweatpants.

"These," she said, "are not for swimming in."

Flip had found an orange T-shirt and scribbled "Bear Bait" on it with a permanent marker.

Sunday looked at it and grinned, but then his eyebrows scrunched up. "Does anyone know what happened to Herod? Is he still on the beach looking for fish?"

"Don't worry about Herod," Flip said. "Eric and Chuck took care of him."

"What do you mean by that?" Sunday asked.

Flip sighed. "Well … you have to remember that Herod wasn't right in the head. We couldn't take any more chances that he was going to hurt someone … or worse."

Suddenly I understood what Flip was saying. I think Sunday did too, because he frowned and shook his head.

Brady put his hand on Sunday's shoulder. "It's okay, Bear Bait. Now maybe we can catch a fish and keep it."

Sunday's mom wagged her finger at the boys. "There will be no more fishing until my boy is well. And then, there will be no more diving in the lake in the dark. Do you understand?"

Sunday nodded while he tried to balance all of his orange things on his lap.

Nurse Diane, the same nurse who had poured brown bottle sting all over Rusty's arm the day before, came out of the hospital doors carrying a clipboard. She snuck up behind Sunday's wheelchair.

"Hey, Mister." Diane kissed the top of Sunday's head. "I hear you're leaving me again."

"You two know each other?" Rusty asked.

Diane tapped the side of her face with her finger.

"Let me see … yeah, I know him. He's only my favorite person in the whole world." She picked up one of Sunday's tangerines and began peeling it. "That's sure a lot of orange stuff you got there."

Sunday laughed. "Diane is my nurse for cancer treatments. She gives the best foot rubs and tells funny jokes. And I like her pretty orange hair."

Diane grabbed her shoulder length ponytail. "I keep telling him, it's auburn."

Sunday shook his head and held the tulips up to Diane's hair. "Orange," he said.

"I thought Sunday went to Missoula for cancer treatments," Mom said.

"I work in both places," Diane said. "Since I live here in Kalispell, I do most of my days here, working in the ER. Two days a week I drive to Missoula to work at the cancer center. That's where I met this crazy young man." She looked back in Sunday's direction. "By the way, I hear you're heading back there in a week or so. I thought we had a deal that you were done with that place."

"It is going to be nothing. You will see."

"Okay. You better not be lying to me."

Another nurse poked her head out the door and called for Diane. She nodded and gave Sunday a hug.

"Gotta go, Handsome. Hey, you're still coming to church on Sunday, right?"

"I would not miss that."

"What's happening at church?" Flip asked.

"I'm getting baptized," Diane said, as she headed back toward the hospital. "And Sunday *has* to be there since he's the one who told me the Good News about Jesus."

"We should all go to church together," Sunday said.

"But first, you must go home and rest," Sunday's mom said.

So we loaded Sunday and all of his orange stuff into Chuck's SUV. The last thing to pack in was his feet, with those orange Riley Mae running shoes on them, as usual.

Sunday's "Good News Shoes."

Chapter 21

"Have you seen Eric?" Flip limped out of the kitchen and into the dining room, holding what looked like a peanut butter and potato chip sandwich. "He's gotta have some of this." He took a bite and rubbed his stomach. "Mmm ... just like when we were kids."

I stared at Flip's horrible sandwich. Peanut butter oozed out on all sides.

"You want some, Riley. You know you do." He grinned and handed me the other half. I don't know why, but I grabbed it and took a big bite. I also got a napkin ready in case I needed something to spit into.

It was crunchy and tasted sweet. And smoky. Not too bad.

"What's in here besides peanut butter and potato chips?"

"Peanut butter cups and bacon," Flip said.

I took another bite. It was yummy. Surprising, coming from Flip.

Eric stumbled in the door, looking upset.

"There's my baby brother," Flip said. "Hungry? I got a great sandwich for you. Riley, give him a bite."

I licked some peanut butter off my fingers. "Sorry." I held my hands up. "All gone."

"Oh good! I'll go make more."

Eric didn't seem interested in a sandwich. "Bro, I need to talk to you." He glanced my way. "Alone."

I jumped to my feet and wiped my hands with a napkin. "I'm outta here. Thanks for the sandwich, Flip. I think I'll make one for Rusty ... as soon as I find her."

Then I left. I walked slowly away, hoping to hear a little of what Eric had to say, but all I heard was, "Drew's back."

"How do you know?"

"I just do. So, what should we do about it?"

Chapter 22

I found Rusty on the phone in our room. I figured she must be talking to her dad.

"Tell him hi for me," I said.

Rusty gave me a funny look. Then she pointed to her phone and mouthed the name "TJ."

My stomach felt a little weird when she said that. It was like having butterflies and cramps at the same time. My palms got sweaty too. I hadn't talked to TJ since before the Half Dome trip, and I knew she was mad at me for missing the softball tournament. Of course, I had no choice, but I couldn't tell her why. For all she knew, I was just her best friend who had been ignoring her.

Before I could think of what to do next, Rusty shoved the phone toward me.

"She wants to talk to you."

Knowing TJ, it was more like she wanted to yell at me. I took the phone, lifting it slowly to my ear. "Hey, TJ."

The girl on the other end of the phone didn't sound at all like my best friend. She sounded ... cheerful.

"Riley! Yay—I finally get to talk to you. What's going on?"

I didn't know what to say. There had been a whole lot going on, and I was starting to get confused about what I could tell and what I couldn't.

"Um ... wow. Lots. We almost got eaten by a bear yesterday."

"That's what Rusty said. Sounds like a 'killer' vacation. And your mom said you were gonna shoot an ad for river sandals in some secret location. Was it fun?"

"Well, I haven't exactly done it yet."

"You guys need to hurry up! I want you to come back here so we can play softball and make brownies. Plus, Breanne's driving me crazy. She talks about Flip like they're dating, ever since we snuck into his office."

"Yeah, I want to come home too. I was really looking forward to having a fun summer."

"If you hurry back you can play All-Stars. We won our first tournament. I struck out fifteen!"

"That's great, TJ. But with the shoe contract and all—"

"The high school coach was there, and he told me that if I keep up the good work, I could start on the varsity team my freshman year. I've been throwing two hundred pitches a night. I bet you can't hit my rise ball at all now."

It seemed like forever since I had played softball. I tried to imagine myself standing in the batter's box, gripping the bat, waiting for TJ's favorite pitch to come flinging out of her hand. In my mind, I hit it over the left field fence.

"We'll see about that," I said.

TJ continued. "Hey—I have all the Riley Mae softball cleats now. You oughta pay me for the publicity." TJ giggled. "Riley? Are you there? Hello?"

"Yeah, I'm here."

"Hello ... hello? Riley, can you hear me?"

It was one of those times when you can hear the other person, but they can't hear you. And then the call was lost.

It was okay. Even though TJ could hear me for a while, I don't think she was listening.

Chapter 23

We all took a couple of days to rest and to get over the shock of the bear scare and the trip to the hospital. The grown-ups spent lots of time reading and napping on lounge chairs in the sun, and the little kids ran around and played ball—except for Sunday, who was allowed to come outside, but had to stay still and warm. Rusty and I did what most girls our age do. We talked, styled each other's hair, watched movies, and snacked on goodies from the kitchen.

"So, what are you gonna do the rest of the summer?" I asked Rusty. We had just put a batch of double-chocolate, chocolate chip cookies in the oven. Rusty invented the recipe with some ingredients we found in the pantry.

Rusty licked the spatula and shook her head. "No idea. I guess help Dad keep the house clean and learn to cook."

"You seem to know what you're doing with these cookies."

"I bake fine, but I burn everything else. Not sure why. What about you? What are you going to do when you get back to Fresno?"

"I dunno. Seems like Swiftriver gets to choose what I do now. I can't believe I begged my parents to sign that contract."

"You think if you didn't have the contract you'd be playing on TJ's All-Star team?"

I thought about that for a minute. The answer was "probably," but I said, "Nah." I don't know why, but I thought that would make Rusty feel better.

"Well, there's no way we could afford for me to play on that team even if I had been invited." Rusty scraped some more batter from the bowl and slurped it up. "Mmm ... these are going to be good."

"Well, I don't know why they didn't invite you to play. You're a really good athlete. And you run so fast! You should be the Riley Mae shoe-girl."

"Except my name's Shari Olivia."

We both looked at each other and laughed.

I had forgotten that Rusty had a real name. "Your initials are S.O.?" That would look cool on the bottom of the shoes. Let's see ... the Shari Olivia Sport Collection, because every girl wants to be S.O. good!"

"Ooh, I like that," Rusty said. "But there can only be one shoe-girl."

Just then the oven timer went off. I grabbed a hot pad

to take the first batch of cookies out of the oven. "Okay, how about you start a cookie company? You could call it S.O. Good."

My dad barged into the kitchen and stood over the pan of cookies. "Are these all for me?"

"You may have one," I said.

Dad took a bite. He pretended to collapse and leaned into the counter. "These cookies are the best I've had in a long time." He took another bite.

I giggled. "That's because of Shari Olivia."

"Who?"

"That's my real name," Rusty said. "But nobody calls me that, ever since that softball practice when the ball went through my legs and the coach said I looked a little 'rusty.'"

"I always wondered where you got that nickname," I said. "I thought maybe it was because of the color of your hair."

Before I could stop him, Dad grabbed three more cookies.

"Dad! Save some for the rest of us!"

"Sorry. I can't help myself!" He took his cookies and ran.

I shook my head. "Sorry about my weird dad."

"It's no trouble." Rusty stepped into the pantry and brought out some new ingredients. "Maybe we can invent some more yummy cookies with this stuff."

For the rest of the afternoon, we experimented with cookies. Some (like the sticky S'more cookies) turned out strange, so we gave them to Flip, who loved them. We ended up making way too many delicious ones (like the oatmeal peanut butter cup cookies), so my mom suggested we box some up to take to church. We decided to make a special gift plate for Diane, with a label on it that said, "Made S.O. good—just for you!"

Chapter 24

The next day was Sunday, and I felt good as my family and I went through the usual "get-ready-for-church routine." It was the first time I had been to church in a few weeks, since all the Swiftriver drama. It wasn't over yet, but at least it had calmed down a little. I didn't know for sure if there were any bad guys still after us, but at least for today, nobody seemed worried about it. I knew that, because Flip and Fawn didn't wear their "disguises." Flip actually showed up dressed in nice, unwrinkled pants and a dress shirt, and Fawn wore a casual pair of khaki capri pants, tan flat sandals and a white blouse. Her smile looked brighter than the blouse. Maybe that was because Matt was holding her hand. I was surprised that Fawn was joining us, since when we first met she told me that she doesn't *go* to church. And Flip—well, he *did* come to church once when I invited him, but he just ate a muffin and left before the service started.

Our group couldn't all fit in Chuck's SUV, so Dad offered to drive our family and Rusty in the red Jeep that belongs to the Stevens' resort.

"Is Sunday coming?" Brady asked.

"Yes," Dad said. "A little later though, toward the end of the service. His parents want him to sleep in a little."

For some reason, I felt a little funny as we pulled into the parking lot of Glacier Christian Church. Maybe it's because I've never gone anywhere but Riverglen Community, or maybe because I knew I wouldn't be seeing TJ or Sean (with my donut). Even though it had only been a few weeks since I'd been at church with them, I wondered if they were going to get used to me not being there and maybe try out the scary youth group and leave me behind as a children's church helper for life.

"Riley." A woman's voice.

"Riley." A man's voice.

"Hey!" My brother's high-pitched squawk pulled me out of my thoughts. "Are you going to answer anybody?"

"Oh, sorry."

"No problem, Honey," Mom said. "We just want to know if you want to take the cookies in now or later."

"We better bring them in now," Rusty said. "Don't want the chocolate chips to melt."

We ended up leaving the cookies in the reception hall, but we brought Diane's gift plate into church with us, so no one would eat her cookies by mistake. I'm not sure that was a good idea, because they smelled so good, I wanted to eat them during the church service.

Focus, Riley.

I normally sit with my parents for the singing and the announcements, and then I go with the kids to children's church during the message. Today, I had to sit through the whole thing. The pastor had been talking about forgiveness and some math problem: seventy times seven. I figured it out in my head. Four-hundred and ninety. We're supposed to forgive that many times, Jesus said. Or maybe he meant more. I wasn't sure about that. I looked at my watch. Eleven o'clock. How long was this message going to last, and more importantly, how long would *I* last with these cookies sitting next to me? My stomach growled. Not one minute longer. I grabbed a cookie and snuck a bite. Rusty giggled.

Brady wasn't distracted at all by the cookies. He was busy drawing Bible maps on the backs of everyone's offering envelopes. Mom grabbed one from Brady to show my dad. "Paul's second missionary journey," she whispered.

Dad shook his head. "Amazing."

"Who's Paul?" Rusty asked.

"He's a guy from the Bible. He traveled around—"

"Shh!" Mom looked at us and pointed toward the pastor, who was smiling right at me and Rusty. I smiled back and then wondered if I had chocolate on my teeth.

"If you have your Bible with you, please turn to Romans, chapter twelve, verses one and two."

I thought at first that the pastor was talking to just me, and I almost said, "okay" out loud. Then I heard pages turning all around me. Of course, he was talking to *everyone* in the church. He just happened to be looking at me when he said it. I looked down and flipped madly through my Bible, hoping that he would choose someone else to stare at before I looked back up again.

"I didn't bring my Bible," Rusty whispered. I knew that at least Rusty had a Bible. A little girl named Ava in our children's church had given Rusty hers when she visited the first time.

I scooted over close to Rusty and let her look on with me.

The pastor began reading, and I made sure to follow along carefully. When the pastor closed his Bible, three people came up the aisle of the church dressed in white robes. A little boy, an older guy with gray hair, and Diane. All of them were smiling big.

When they got to the front of the church, the pastor led them through a door on the side of the stage, and they all disappeared for a minute. Then the back of the stage opened up, and they appeared again, standing on a platform that had steps that led down into a clear-sided pool.

Brady stood up and looked around. "Where's Sunday?"

Mom pulled him back down onto his seat.

"But she's getting baptized now, and he's not here."

We all looked around then, but we didn't stand up like Brady did. I didn't see Sunday or his family anywhere.

I admit that I didn't pay any attention to what the little boy and the gray-haired man said before they got dunked. People took pictures and clapped after each one, but that's all I noticed. I was too busy worrying that Sunday was going to miss Diane getting baptized.

Then Rusty pointed to the front. There was Sunday, holding a microphone!

"What's he doing up there?" Brady asked.

"Shhh, just listen," Mom said.

Sunday smiled real big and took a piece of paper out of the pocket of his orange sweat pants. Yes, he was wearing the orange shoes too.

Before he started reading, he said: "This next person is my good friend, Diane. God brought her to me as my nurse when I was in the hospital. She asked me to read a story of how Jesus saved her life."

Jesus saved her life? That had my attention.

Sunday began reading while Diane stood in the water with the pastor. Even though it was Sunday's voice, I could imagine Diane talking . . .

"My name is Diane, and I have always believed in God. But I thought he didn't like me much. Maybe it was because

116

my parents got divorced when I was young. I figured that God didn't think I was good enough to have a happy family. So, for most of my childhood, I thought I was a bad person, and then in my teen years, I chose to do some things that were bad just to prove myself right. One of the things I did was to abuse alcohol, and I soon became an alcoholic. My addiction destroyed my life. I lost my family, my friends, and everything good ..."

I looked around the church. Everyone was silent, and all eyes were fixed on Diane, who had tears streaming down her face.

Sunday continued reading:

"Thankfully, the God I believed in as a kid really did exist. And I found out that not only did he like me—he loved me! One day, when I had run away from everyone and everything, I ended up in a Dairy Queen here in Montana, of all places. A nice couple named Chuck and Carmie noticed that I looked lost, and they offered me a place to stay for a while until I could get my life back on track. They invited me to attend a recovery group at this church, and after I had been sober for a few months, they offered to help me through nursing school."

Rusty nudged me and whispered, "Lucky Chuck." I smiled and nodded.

"As good as that sounds, the best was yet to come. After I became a nurse, I met a young man from Africa named Sunday."

Sunday stopped reading for a minute and said, "That is me." He smiled and laughed his contagious Sunday laugh, which made the church laugh too. Sunday's mom gave him a stern look and pointed to the paper he was supposed to be reading.

He smiled again and continued.

"Sunday shared the Good News with me, and I finally asked Jesus into my heart. You see, here was a boy who had a tough childhood like I had. His parents weren't divorced like mine, but he had leukemia—a serious illness that could take his life at any time. And even though he was suffering, inside I could tell that he had a peace that could not be taken away by anything. He said it was because of Jesus. He also told me that Jesus wanted to give me that same peace."

I looked over at Rusty and noticed she was catching tears dripping off her chin.

"So, here I am today, to be baptized, and to tell all of you that I love Jesus. My life isn't perfect, and I still do bear pain from the consequences of my sinful life, but I know that God has forgiven me through Jesus and that he has made me into a new person."

Sunday folded up the paper and scanned the crowd. We were all still. It was like we wanted to hear more. "That is all," he said, and he sat down on the front of the stage.

The pastor spoke. "Diane, because of your profession of faith in Jesus as your Lord and Savior, I now baptize you in the name of the Father, the Son, and the Holy Spirit."

Diane held her nose as the pastor pushed her backwards into the water. Because of the clear panels surrounding the pool, we could see her when she was all the way under. Her rust-colored hair spread out and swirled all over, and her eyes were closed. Then she popped back up, pushed her hair back from her face and let out a huge "Woo-hoo!"

Next thing, we heard a splash. An "orange" kid had joined the celebration in the pool.

Sunday's mother covered her face with her hands and shook her head.

Maybe she should have brought Sunday some orange swim trunks.

Chapter 25

"Wow—that was some story." Mom brushed a few tears from her face as we gathered our belongings.

Chuck and Carmie came over to greet us.

"Did you guys really pay for Diane to go to nursing school?" I asked. "Are *you* rich too?"

"Riley, don't be so nosy," Mom said.

Chuck patted my mom on the shoulder. "I'm glad she asked. It gives me a chance to give God some more glory. Back a long time ago, we scraped up some change and invested in a little piece of property in Wyoming. Seems it had a little flow of oil under it."

Carmie crossed her arms and raised her eyebrows. "A little oil?"

"Ha!" Chuck slapped his knee. "It's been flowin' for twenty years or so."

"Wow—you *are* lucky." I said.

"Nah, just blessed that God trusted this old cowboy with the resources."

"I'm gonna go find Sunday," Brady said. "I'm gonna give him my dry shoes." Then he disappeared. Wow, that was nice of my brother.

We all gathered in the reception hall of the church to wait for the newly baptized people to dry off and join us for cookies and lemonade. The little boy came in first, and the crowd all applauded for him. He smiled at me. He was missing his two front teeth.

"He must be a second grader," I said to Rusty.

The old guy came in next, and when he smiled, he didn't have front teeth either.

Rusty looked at me and we both whispered it at the same time.

"Second grader."

Diane was the last to come in. She had dried her hair, and it shined as it rested in soft curls just on top of her shoulders. Her cheeks were all pink, and her eyes sparkled. She jumped a little and waved. "Hi, everybody."

We all rushed forward and got in line for hugs, and when Rusty and I finally got ours, we gave her the gift plate of cookies. "Oh, wow. These look great," she said, and she lifted the wrap off the top, grabbed one, and took a big bite. "Yum. Who made these?"

I pointed my thumb at Rusty. "Shari Olivia," I said.

Diane started to choke. I wasn't surprised, that bite had been huge.

"Are you okay?" Matt asked. He looked ready to proceed with the Heimlich maneuver.

Diane nodded and then ran for the lemonade table. She took a big swig of drink and leaned over, her hands on the table.

"I hate when food goes down the wrong way," I said.

"Yeah," Mom said. "Why don't you girls go find Brady and Sunday? I'll go make sure Diane's okay. Maybe she can join us for lunch back at the Stevens' place."

We didn't have to look for the boys, because right then they ran into the reception hall and raided the cookie table.

"I'm starving!" Sunday said. He shoved a bite of chocolate, chocolate chip cookie into his mouth. "I'm embarrassed to have slept through breakfast. When is lunch?"

Chapter 26

Lunch was ready as soon as we arrived back home at the Stevens' resort. Someone had prepared a huge buffet of barbequed chicken, potato salad, corn on the cob, rolls, watermelon, and chocolate cake.

Sunday was the first in line to fill his plate, and I was glad to see him eat as much as he wanted.

"Why is Diane not here?" Sunday asked my mom.

"I think she was tired from working so much and wanted an afternoon to rest," Mom said. "She thanked me for the invitation and asked if she could take us up on it another time."

"Well, I'm glad it wasn't because she hated the cookies," Rusty said.

"Aack! The cookies! I'll be right back." I had forgotten to take the leftover cookies out of the Jeep when we got home after church. I ran to get the keys from Dad.

But the Jeep wasn't where Dad had parked it when we got home. Rats. I scanned the front of the Stevens' property and finally spotted the Jeep over by the horse barns. It wasn't too far, so I decided to jog over in my own pair of orange running shoes. Didn't want Sunday having all the fun. As I got closer, I noticed a man in a cowboy hat talking to Eric. So, Eric was the Jeep and cookie snatcher!

I thought about running up behind him to flick his ear and give him a hard time about missing church, but it looked to me like the man in the hat was getting a little angry. I watched as he shoved his finger into Eric's chest a couple of times, and then I slowed way down and ducked behind the side of the barn so they couldn't see me. Eric pushed the man away, but the man charged back and slammed his fist down on the hood of the Jeep. Whoa—that would leave a dent. Eric made some gesture with his hands, kinda like a softball umpire does when you're safe on base, and then the man stomped away, out of my view. I heard an engine rev up—a motorcycle or something—and then the sound faded in the distance. I peeked out from behind the barn and saw Eric get in the Jeep and start it up.

"Hey! My cookies!" I stood there and watched as Eric peeled out and left a cloud of dirt as he sped down the road that exited the Stevens' property.

Chapter 27

Rusty teased me when I returned to the group with no cookies. "You ate them, I know you did."

"It is okay, there is plenty of cake." Sunday went back for *another* piece.

"I think he has a special stomach just for dessert," I said to Rusty.

"Who's up for a competitive round of volleyball?" Fawn had changed from her church outfit to some cute athletic clothes, and she tossed a bright orange ball to Matt.

"Only if I'm on your team," he said.

"I'm out," Flip said, pointing to his ankle cast.

"Me too." Rusty held up her stitched arm. "Actually, I think I'd like to go read in our room for a while."

"Sunday may *not* play," Sunday's mom said.

We decided the teams would be me and Dad against Matt and Fawn. Sunday's sisters and Flip wanted to be the cheerleaders, and Mom, of course, was the referee.

Brady grabbed Sunday by the arm. "Let's go play video games."

Sunday looked at his mom, and she nodded her head. Then he smiled and disappeared with my brother.

"Haven't you forgotten something?" Flip pointed over to the sand volleyball court, which had two poles sticking up, but no net strung between them.

"Where do we keep the net?" Fawn asked.

"Right there on the poles, usually," Flip said.

"Well, it's not there."

"No kidding, I was the one who pointed that out. Maybe Chuck stored it someplace for the winter." Flip pushed himself up from his lounge chair, but Matt motioned for him to sit back down.

"I'll go find him. Be right back."

Matt did come back after a while, but with no net. "Chuck doesn't know where it is. If you guys still want to play, we could tie a rope or something across."

By then, Fawn had gotten all comfortable on a lounge chair under a shady tree.

"I think I'll take a nap instead, and dream that I'm an Olympic volleyball star and I'm whooping you all in the gold medal round." She smiled and closed her eyes.

"Well, I can't let her have all the fun," Matt said. He spread a blanket out on the ground and lay down. "We're attacking the river tomorrow, so a little rest might be just what's needed." Soon after that, Mom and Dad were snoozing on lounges and Sunday's family had disappeared somewhere.

Flip and I sat there, staring at each other.

"Are you tired?" Flip asked me.

"Nope," I said.

"So, what do you want to do?"

"Can you play ping-pong with that bad ankle?"

Flip grinned. "Girl, you *don't* even know."

Chapter 28

It turns out that Flip is some kind of national ping-pong champion. He claimed that he couldn't find his trophy to prove it, but even if he was just kidding, it didn't matter, because he really could play. I didn't even score a point in the first game.

"You serve too hard!" I ran to the corner of the room to retrieve one of the ping-pong balls that had ricocheted off the table and then off my forearm.

"Hard, shmard," Flip said. "You need to toughen up for your river trip."

"C'mon, just serve *one* easy so I can hit it back to you."

"Oh, okaaaay." Flip delivered the next serve in slow motion, and I finally was able to return the ball. Then his eyes widened as he smacked it super hard again, and it bounced off the table and into my lower lip.

"Owwww!" I immediately felt a bump raise up where my lip got smashed between the ball and my tooth.

Flip frowned and hobbled over to my side of the table.

"Oh, hey, I'm sorry, kiddo. The ball wasn't supposed to hit you in the mouth." He put his hand on my shoulder and looked me in the eyes, pouting a bit. Then his Flip-smirk appeared. "You do know that was game point."

That did it. Who cares about a little fat lip?

"Oh, good." I said. "Let's play again. Now it's *my* serve, and I'm on to your little game."

I wound up like I was going to hit my serve really hard. Flip stood back from the table, getting ready to return it. Instead of whacking it, I tapped it easy, and it landed on Flip's side of the table, close to the net. He lunged, but missed it.

"Nice whiff! That makes the score 1-0, and I serve again." I blew on the ball and gave Flip the evil eye.

This time I executed a perfect softball-windmill-arm serve. Flip lunged forward, but I hit the ball way up in the air, and it came down and bounced off his head, and out of bounds.

"Pretty sneaky," Flip said.

"Looks like the national champ's a little confused. Two, zip!"

I blew on the ball. Gave the evil eye again … and then I totally ran out of ideas! It wasn't fair. I hardly ever play ping-pong. So, in my confusion, I ended up tapping the ball over the net, which must have made it look as big as a meatball to Flip, who pounded it. But this time it didn't hit me, because I dove under the table.

I heard the ball ricochet off one wall, and then another, and then it splashed in something.

"Wow! I couldn't do that again if I tried. One to two," Flip said.

I poked my head up just far enough for Flip to see my eyes, glaring at him.

"C'mon, Riley. You can't play from under there."

I stood up and stuck out my fat boo-boo lip. "How about you play with your left hand?"

Flip tossed the paddle in the air. It turned over a couple of times, and then he snatched the handle with his left hand. "I've been hoping you'd ask that."

I forgot Flip was left-handed.

And then the serves came harder, except for when he faked a hard serve and then dribbled it. One time he let me get a few volleys in, but then he wound up, and after I dove under the table, he hit a gentle one.

Flip laughed so hard one time that he completely missed the ball when he tried to serve.

"My serve! My serve!" I danced around the table.

This time, I didn't even try to hit the table. I just batted the ball straight at Flip.

The ball smacked him right on the lower lip. I watched as a little bump appeared immediately where his lip got smashed between the ball and his tooth.

We both collapsed on the ground laughing. For a minute I thought I might wet my pants.

"What is wrong with you two?" I looked up from the ground to see Sunday, shaking his head. Both Sunday and Brady stared down at us like we were crazy.

Flip still lay on the floor laughing. "Just a little friendly game of ping-pong," he said. "You guys wanna play?"

Brady's eyes flicked back and forth between Flip's and my fat lip, kinda like he was watching a tennis match. "No, it looks too dangerous. Come on, Sunday, let's go finish blowing up those aliens."

Flip rubbed his lip and collapsed laughing on the floor again. "What do you say we call it a tie and go get some ice for these injuries?"

Chapter 29

The ice helped relieve the pain, but I wanted to check out the damage in a mirror. I cracked open the door to the dark bedroom, and I found Rusty, laying on her bed. She jumped up when she saw the bag of ice on my mouth.

"A ping-pong ball did that?" Rusty dug some sparkly, purple lip gloss out of her backpack. "Here, now nobody will know."

I uncapped the gloss and spread it on my lips. It hurt a little when I rolled it over the bruise. "So, what have you been up to while I've been getting beat up by the Ping-Pong Champ of the World?"

Rusty sat back down on her bed and smiled. "Um ... I just asked Jesus into my heart."

"What?"

"Well, I've been thinking about it for a while. And then, today, I heard what Diane said at the baptism, about how she used to think God didn't like her very much."

I plopped down on my bed and shook my head. "I know. How could she believe such a silly thing?"

Rusty stood up. "But Riley, that's *exactly* what I always thought too, since my mom left and all."

"Seriously?" I sat back up. "You thought that God didn't like you?"

Rusty looked at me and nodded.

"Wait," I said. "*When* did you do this?"

"When did I do what?" Rusty looked confused.

"Ask Jesus into your heart."

"A little while ago. I was sitting in that beanbag chair over there, and—"

"I don't think you can do that."

"What?"

"Become a Christian while I'm playing ping-pong."

Rusty crossed her arms. "Well, apparently I can, because I did."

"But, I wasn't here with you."

"It's *okay*, Riley. It was something I needed to do by myself. You've been here *for* me, and it's because of you that I even heard about Jesus in the first place."

"Oh." I didn't know what else to say.

Rusty plunked down in the beanbag chair. "But I have to admit, I've been a little confused. Your family seems, well, perfect I guess, so I figured that Jesus wouldn't be interested in a messed-up person like me."

"You think our family is perfect? That's funny. You *have* seen me and Brady fight, right?"

Rusty laughed. "Yeah."

"And I get grouchy sometimes."

Rusty held her hand up in the air. "Riley, I get it now. *No one* is perfect. And that's why Jesus died—to take the punishment we each deserve for all of our sins."

We both sat there, quiet for a moment. I lay down on the bed and looked up at the ceiling. "So ... you really asked him in? While I was playing ping-pong?"

"Yep. And now I really want to find my mom, so I can tell her about Jesus."

I sat up, rubbed my lip, and looked down at my Riley Mae running shoes.

Maybe this contract thing wasn't such a big mistake after all.

I thought about all that had happened to bring Rusty and me together as friends. It probably wouldn't have happened at all if I hadn't started working for Swiftriver, which caused our softball team to need a shortstop to take my place. And before all the drama on Half Dome, I had been trying to figure out how to wear the "Good News Shoes" that the Bible teaches about in Ephesians 6:15—and to share with Rusty how she could have peace with God through Jesus. But then the accident happened and we flew to Montana and everything got messed up.

Or did it?

Rusty stood up and came over to sit with me on my bed. "Riley? Will you help me find my mom?"

I smiled. I put my arm around Rusty and gave her a big squeeze. "Yeah. I don't really know how yet, but yeah."

God, please help me know what to do. Rusty needs her mom.

I thought about my own mom, and how she's been there for me my whole life. Our hallway at home is filled with pictures of me and her every year on my first day of school—standing next to her police car, which also happened to be my ride.

That gave me an idea. "Hey Rusty, do you have a picture of your mom?"

"Just one." Rusty unlatched a chain from around her neck. She pulled a locket out from under her shirt and opened it.

"You've had her picture with you this whole time? We can probably look her up on the Internet or something!"

Too bad the picture was so teeny. All I could make out was a person with reddish hair, holding a baby who must have been Rusty.

I squinted at the picture. "I can hardly see her face at all! This could be *my* mom. Or Fawn. Actually, if Matt grew his hair out a little more, it could be him." I giggled. "Are you sure this isn't your dad?"

Rusty grabbed the locket back from me. "Hey, quit making fun. It's all I have."

"I'm sorry. It's a nice picture, but we *have* to find another one. Maybe you could ask your dad—"

"Nope. Not gonna do that."

"Okay. Then we'll have to find her another way."

"I've been praying," Rusty said.

"That'll work." I punched her in the arm and smiled. "Christian."

Chapter 30

The river was cold. No one warned me about that.

"Do you really expect me to get in here? I can't swim if my arms and legs are frozen, you know." I stood at the edge of the river and pretended to do a freestyle stroke, but with stiff arms. "See?"

"Riley, quit being so dramatic and get up here and help us." Mom had her hands on her hips. She, Fawn, and Matt stood by the van that held our raft on the roof. I guess they expected me to help carry the big old thing down the hill. Rusty and Flip weren't going to be any help with their injuries. Flip had asked Rusty to follow him on foot along the river and be his photography assistant today. Since Flip was still struggling with that cast, he planned to have her haul the equipment while he limped along down the riverbank. It didn't sound like a lot of fun for Rusty, but at least she wouldn't get wet.

Matt positioned all four of us on one side of the van. "Okay," he said, "on the count of three, we're going to pull the raft off the van halfway. Then, Fawn and I will get under it, and walk our hands over to the other side as you two pull it off the van the rest of the way. The goal is to end up with the raft over our heads. If you get tired, let it rest on your head. Then we'll count to three again, and at the same time, we'll move out from under the raft and let her down gently to the ground. "

"Sounds like an instant headache," I said.

"Good thing you had that ping-pong training," Flip said. "You're ready for anything now."

"Tell me you didn't play ping-pong with him," Fawn said.

"Oh yeah, I did. I have this purple lip as proof."

Fawn grimaced. "I've had many lips like that myself."

"Okay," Matt yelled. "Here we go. One, two ..."

I reached up toward the raft, but my arms were too short to even touch it.

Uh-oh.

"Three!"

All I heard next was a bunch of ladies screaming.

"I don't have it!"

"Whoops!"

"It's not working!"

Then, the raft fell to the ground. Dust kicked up all around us. We sputtered and coughed. When the dust settled, we watched as Matt climbed out from under the raft. He looked like a sandman.

"Okay then," he said, as he spit some dirt out of his mouth. "Let's take her down to the water, shall we?"

We all grabbed a handle from each of the four corners of the raft, and we slid and tripped down the hill toward the river. I tried my best to carry my end of the back of the raft, but that thing was heavy. A couple of times I dropped my handle and the raft dragged. I also couldn't see what was in front of me, so I accidently kicked a rock with my big toe. Ouch. The most annoying thing about that was that I was sure it scraped off some of my glittery, gold toenail polish that I had put on the night before to go with my new Ready Eddy river sandals.

When we finally made it down to the water, I dunked my toe in. To numb it mostly, which worked in that cold water. I also wanted to assess the damage to my pedicure. Just as I thought, the whole big toe was missing polish. And the toenail was chipped.

Great.

Flip and Rusty took pictures of us as we put on our life vests and helmets.

"Don't photograph my toe, please. It looks nasty. And, why do we need these helmets?" I hoisted on my vest, which smelled weird to me. "Did a fish wear this last?"

Rusty sniffed the vest and crinkled up her nose. "Sorry about the toe. Luckily, this is only a practice photo shoot."

I looked down at Rusty's nice, polished gold toenails. Since she was originally scheduled to be on this shoot with us, she had on a pair of Ready Eddys too.

"Hey, Flip, you can photograph Rusty's toes and paste them on my legs for the pictures since hers look better."

Matt handed us all paddles. "Can we stop talking about toes for just a minute so I can give you some instruction?"

Matt assigned us special positions in the raft. Fawn was placed up front in the center, and Mom and I took our places in the second row—me on the left, Mom on the right. Matt was in the middle in the back.

The first thing I did wrong was that I sat down in the bottom of the raft.

"You need to sit on the side and tuck your feet under that middle part at the bottom." Matt had to be kidding. How was sitting on the side of the raft supposed to keep me *in* it?

"Let's try an easy command," Matt said. "When I call, 'All forward,' I want you to paddle forward. Make sure you get your paddle in the water and really dig in. That's what's going to keep your body in the raft."

I learned from the Half Dome hike that Matt really knows what he's talking about, so I tried to stay focused and do what he asked so I would stay safe. Matt said to dig, so I did. But we weren't in the water, so I dug a hole in the dirt.

"Riley, you don't have to actually dig yet," Matt said. "This is just practice."

"Oh, sorry."

"No problem. Let's try another one. All back!"

We pretended to paddle backward, but I didn't dig this time.

"Hey, this is easy," I said.

"Oh yeah, well how about this? Right forward, left back!"

I had to think about that for a minute, but I got it. I was on the left, so I was supposed to paddle backward.

"What should I do?" Fawn was sitting in the middle of the front seat.

"Get on Mrs. Hart's side. I'll stay over here with Riley. That should even out the sides."

"Won't that spin us in circles?" I asked.

"Yep," Matt said. "That's the fun of it. You don't need to worry, Riley. This is an easy trip. "

"Excuse me," Flip said, "But this is making for some pretty boring pictures. When do you try it in the water?"

"Patience, man. We have one more command to learn. It's one of the most important."

All this dusty paddling was making me hot and thirsty. The river water actually looked inviting to me now, so I determined to listen to Matt so we could get on with the show.

"When I call, 'Get down,' I want you all to kneel down

and get as low as you can in the bottom of the raft. Duck your heads down and hold your paddle next to you, with the handle part pointing up. Grab one of the raft straps with your other hand and hang on."

"When are we going to have to do that?" I asked.

"When we go over the waterfalls," Matt said. "I'll stay up on the back of the raft and guide us down."

Waterfalls? I immediately thought of Vernal Falls that we had just hiked up in Yosemite. And Niagara Falls.

"I'm sorry," I said, "but I don't think I can do waterfalls."

"These aren't big waterfalls. Still, I don't want you ladies falling out of the raft."

"So, what if we do?" Mom asked.

"If you fall out, hang on to your paddle, point your feet downstream, and pretend you're sitting in a lounge chair. You'll bounce off the rocks fairly gently. I'll try to get to you and pull you into the raft, but if I can't, just relax, and when the white water stops you'll be able to swim to the shore, where the eddy is."

"What's an eddy again?" I knew Matt told me before at one of our meetings, but I forgot. Or maybe I was more interested in remembering now since I might have to swim to one.

"It's where the current goes the opposite way from the rest of the water."

"Just think," Fawn said, "you gotta go against the flow."

"Oh. Okay. Because the flow is going down the water-fall, right? Hey, what if I go down a waterfall without the raft?"

"You won't," Matt said. "But *if* you do, curl up into a ball, take a deep breath, and relax. The water will pull you down under for a little while, but you'll eventually pop back up."

"Like a ping-pong ball," Flip laughed. Then he snapped a picture of me.

"Right into your lip," I said.

"Ooh," Fawn said, "I'd like a picture of that."

Our "dry run" was now over, so after waiting a few minutes for Flip and Rusty to hike to the first lookout, we finally got to shove off. I put my hand over the side of the raft and grabbed a handful of water to splash on my dusty legs. They cleaned off nicely, but unfortunately, my feet were covered in mud.

"Hey, how are we gonna get any good pictures of my feet when they look like this?"

"Don't worry," Matt said. "Morning Coffee will wash everything off."

"Morning Coffee?"

"Yeah. Can't you hear it brewing? All forward!"

It turns out that "Morning Coffee" was the name of our first rapid. They call it that because the freezing water slaps you in the face and wakes you right up.

Unfortunately, when that happened, I was so shocked that I didn't follow Matt's instructions.

"Uh, girls?" Matt said. "No one paddled through that rapid."

My face was frozen, and since my mouth had dropped open right before the wave hit me, it was full of icy river water. So I choked my answer.

"It's ... c-c-cold!" I looked over at Mom and Fawn. They didn't have a dry place on them. Fawn was shivering, but at least she was smiling. Mom, on the other hand, looked like a cat that had been dunked in a bathtub by surprise.

"Was that a Class Four?" I asked Matt.

Matt threw his head back and laughed. "That was barely a Class One! Maybe you should have stayed home and sipped tea today."

"Nonsense," Fawn said. "Now that we've had our morning coffee, we're ready to roll. Right ladies?" She sat up straighter on her side of the raft. "What's next?"

I wasn't ready to roll. But I was in the raft, and the only way to get out of "what was next" was to leave the raft, and I never intended to do that—ever.

"The next rapid," Matt said, "is called Break Neck."

"Lovely." Mom still looked a little rattled.

"It gets its name because the water is shallow, and that causes the raft to skid over several rocks. Our heads are going to bounce around like we're human bobbleheads. We *all* have to paddle hard to keep us from stalling in the middle. If we stall, we'll have to get out and push the raft."

This time when I heard Matt's "All forward" command, I paddled as hard as I could. And then I saw Fawn's head bobbing up and down, which was hilarious, so I stopped paddling for a minute to look over at Mom.

"R-i-i-i-i-l-l-l-e-e-e-y! P-a-a-a-d-d-d-l-l-l-e!" She babbled as she bobbled.

"O-o-o-h, y-e-e-a-a-h," I babbled back.

We stalled. Uh-oh.

Water continued to rush hard on both sides. I could feel the raft lifting up behind us. I glanced back in time to see Matt, standing outside of the raft, pushing the back end.

"All forward!" he yelled.

I tried. But my paddle hit rocks. Same thing must've happened to Mom and Fawn, because we didn't go anywhere.

"We can't!" I yelled back.

"Then bounce up and down, and I'll keep pushing." Hmm. Bouncing. I could do that.

As soon as I started seriously bouncing, the raft lurched forward, and we were free. But then Matt bounced down the center of the raft and almost knocked Fawn into the water. He gently lifted her up by the arm.

"Sorry about that," Matt said. "I had to dive in the raft so you ladies wouldn't go down the river without me." Matt helped Fawn back to her seat, kneeled down, and looked into her eyes. "Are you hurt?"

"I'm fine." Fawn blushed. She picked up her paddle. "Thanks for the help. When do we get to the hard stuff?"

Fawn is so tough.

"Now," Matt said.

Chapter 31

The Tube Chute was next on the agenda. Our first waterfall. And, unfortunately, the biggest one.

"How come we have to start with the hardest?" I asked.

Matt pointed to the sky. "Ask the River-maker. Now, ladies, I need you to paddle hard, and then you're going to get down in the bottom of the raft."

My adrenaline kicked in and I started to paddle like crazy.

"Not yet, Riley," Mom said.

"Oh, sorry." I looked up ahead and noticed that the river began to narrow. Water flowed in at us from both sides. All I saw in front of us were rocks.

"All forward!" Matt yelled. I hoped he had a magic steering wheel in the back of the raft, 'cause he needed to turn us to the right ... fast.

I paddled with all my might, even as waves of water slapped me in the face. Somehow we made the turn.

"Get down!" Matt yelled again.

I flattened myself like a pancake on the bottom of the raft. If Flip was taking pictures, he wouldn't get me in them. No chance I was flying out. I dared to look up, though, and realized that I held the flat part of my paddle up in the air. Rats, I did it wrong. Flip would get a picture of *that* and tease me about it for days.

"Get ready for a bump!" Matt yelled.

Bump? I raised up to look. He never said anything about a—

"Hang on!" Fawn grabbed the back of my vest and pulled me down.

A huge rock appeared right in front of our raft. Well, it didn't *just* appear, it had always been there, our raft was just being propelled right into it.

We bumped it. Hard. Then we got *stuck* on it.

"High side!" Matt shouted, as water swirled all around, pinning us to the rock. I looked back and saw him standing on the right side of the raft, rocking it. Mom jumped up and joined Matt—and then Fawn too. I held my ground as the "raft pancake."

In seconds, the raft was loose from the rock and Matt yelled again. "Get down!"

I, of course, was already down, but I did switch my paddle so the correct end was up. Perfect.

And that's when someone—I guess it was the "River-maker"—took the ground out from under us, and we plunged downward. At the bottom, the raft went totally underwater, and that meant that I did too. It felt a little like the time I first learned to body surf at the beach. I tumbled around in the waves and drank half the ocean. Only this time, the water wasn't salty, so it tasted better. The choking fit felt the same though. Water flew out my nose, which would have been embarrassing except that the same thing happened to Mom and Fawn. Matt sat on the back of the raft and laughed.

"That was the best!" he said.

"Um," I choked out the words with about a gallon of the river, "you didn't tell us about that rock, or about what 'high side' means. But now I know why we need helmets."

"Yes," Fawn said. "But Matt had it under control the whole time. Wasn't it exciting, Riley?" Then she stood up, stretched, and waved to Flip and Rusty, who were sitting at the edge of the river. The water had calmed, and the sun beat down on us, taking my river-water shivers away.

I like calm waters.

Chapter 32

I wish I could say we were done for the day, but no. We still had the Butter-Churn rapids and the Get-Out-Now rapids to go. Both were easy to maneuver compared to our adventure down the Tube Chute. There was only one catch to the Get-Out-Now rapids. They flowed over an eight-foot waterfall, and right after that was the Thrill-and-Kill. The Thrill-and-Kill was a Class Six rapid that was considered impossible to run.

"Some of the more experienced guides go through and make it," Matt said, "but it's a fifteen-foot waterfall with more than a few rocks at the bottom, so we'll be getting out. There's a nice eddy at the bottom of Get-Out-Now."

"Matt, what if I fall out of the raft on the rapids and can't get to the eddy?"

"You won't fall out, Miss Pancake. And if you do, you *will* be able to get to the eddy. Just swim as hard as you can."

"DON'T miss the eddy." Mom's stern glare sent fearful chills up my spine. Worse than river-water chills.

It turned out not to be a problem. The rapids were actually fun. The water slapped me in the face a couple of times, but I really enjoyed the falls. I found myself wishing we could go back and do Get-Out-Now again. The water current and the curve of the river directed our raft to the eddy without any effort on our part.

"That was awesome," I said later, after Flip and Rusty had caught up with us on the side of the river.

"Then why didn't you smile?" Flip scrolled through the digital pictures on his camera. "I got so many good shots, but you're frowning in every one."

"It's a little hard to smile when water is slapping you in the mouth."

"Well, I guess we'll have to practice that later with the water hose." Flip grinned. "Gotta have some smiles by Friday."

I turned to Matt. "We're doing the shoot in two days?"

"I don't see why not. I like how the water is running now. If we wait too long, the levels might change, which makes it a whole new river."

"I wish I wasn't flying out on Friday." Rusty frowned and sat down next to me on the side of the raft.

What Rusty didn't know yet, but all the rest of us did, was that Rusty's dad was actually the one flying out on Friday. He was flying out of Fresno—to come and surprise Rusty in Montana.

Chapter 33

Good news and bad news awaited us back at the Stevens' resort. The good news was that Tyler (the somersaulting pilot) had called Eric to tell him that everything had checked out with the busted landing gear on the jet.

"Yeah, Ty says something just locked up. Says that we ought to stop buying jets on clearance and get some good ones for a change." Eric, who I last saw in some kind of argument with a stranger, seemed relaxed and relieved.

Mom looked confused and suspicious. "Really? The last time he spoke with my detectives, he had a different story."

"Yeah, he said he tried to call you but didn't get an answer. I'm sure he left a message on your phone. How was the river? Did you like the Tube Chute?"

Mom poked some numbers on her phone. "Like isn't quite the word. I'll be glad when Riley's finished with the river sandal campaign." She put the phone to her ear for a minute, then scrunched her eyebrows together. "Hmm. Nothing from Tyler. I think I'll give him a quick call—"

"Oh no!" Flip, who had been talking on his phone, interrupted us all with the bad news of the day. "Sunday's been admitted to the cancer center in Missoula. He may have pneumonia, and his numbers are low."

"What does that mean?" I asked.

"The leukemia might be back. That poor kid and his family have been through so much! I have to get down there."

How could Sunday be worse? We'd been praying for him to get better.

God, aren't you listening?

Mom called Dad and found out that he and Brady were already on their way to Missoula, a two-hour drive from the Stevens' resort. Brady wanted to see his friend and take him an orange smoothie to help "cool his fever."

Flip fumbled around on the counter and came up with a set of car keys. "Eric, where's the Jeep?"

Eric shrugged. "Mr. Hart took it."

"Have you seen Chuck? I need to borrow his SUV."

"Chuck's out too."

Flip slammed the keys back on the counter. "Then make yourself useful for a change and get me another car, okay?"

It was the first time I ever saw Flip mad. Or frustrated. Or impatient. Or whatever he was. I felt a little sorry for Eric, who got the bad end of it.

"So sorry to let you down, Mr. Stevens." Eric stood up and bowed to Flip. "Would you like me to call a limo?"

"If that's all you know how to do, then yes."

Fawn broke up the brotherly "love." "Flip—you can't go anywhere looking like that. You're all sandy and gross. They won't let you in to see Sunday with all that dirt on you. Go clean up and I'll take care of this."

Flip grumbled something about how hard it is to clean up with a cast on his foot, and then he dragged himself off to his room.

Fawn dug her phone out of her bag and made a quick call. "Yes, I was wondering if I could rent a car and have it delivered to me. How much is the extra charge? That won't be a problem. Thanks. Sure, let me get my credit card."

Eric stormed out of the room.

"Well," Mom said. "Seems we can't do too much for Sunday right at this minute, and you all must be starved. Let's go get some food."

She led the way into the kitchen. I *was* starved, but I also felt sick about Sunday. I sat down on a stool, crossed my arms on the counter, and laid my head down.

Lord, please help him be okay.

Rusty disappeared into the pantry and came out with

the only thing that I could even think about swallowing at a time like this. A double-chocolate, chocolate chip cookie.

"Thanks, friend," I said.

"You're welcome. Chocolate heals, you know."

I looked down at Rusty's torn-up arm, and it looked better. I pointed to it. "I think you've been sneaking your fair share of the cookies."

"Oops." She looked at her arm and patted her stomach. "Yeah. I'm guilty."

In fact, everything about Rusty looked better. She smiled brighter and her eyes sparkled. Her face glowed—although I'm sure that had something to do with getting too much sun out on the river. But besides that, she had seemed much more peaceful the last couple of days.

And *that* wasn't from eating chocolate.

Chapter 34

I was tired from the thrill of rafting. Mom and Fawn were too. So even though we really wanted to see Sunday and his family at the cancer center, we decided it would be best if we girls stayed home.

After Flip and Eric left for Missoula, Matt stood around for a minute, staring at us. Then he glanced down at his fancy sport watch. "Well, it looks like it may be time for you ladies to have tea, so I'm going to tend to the rafting equipment and maybe go for a hike, or do something else, uh ... outside." He backed up and disappeared out the door.

"Tea?" Mom laughed and looked at Fawn. "I'm thinking a nap would be better."

Fawn stretched and yawned. "Oh yeah."

Rusty and I didn't feel like sleeping, so we started all over again with my pedicure. After my toes were all shiny and new again, we brainstormed ways to find Rusty's mom.

"I can't believe there isn't a computer anywhere in this place," Rusty said.

"Oh, I'm sure one of them has a laptop hidden around here," I said. "If I only knew where ..."

I stood up, with cotton still between my toes and walked down the hallway, peeking in bedrooms.

Rusty followed me down the hall. "Riley, don't *even* think about it," she whispered.

Of course I didn't think about it. If I had, I would have had to turn back around. But then we wouldn't have found the computer!

Flip's bedroom door was half-open, so I walked in. His laptop sat on the floor, next to his bed. And ... it was already on and connected to a network.

"Rusty, quick," I whisper-yelled, "come in and close the door."

"No," she said, although she was already standing next to me, *and* she had already closed the door.

"This will only take a minute." I pulled up the search engine on Flip's computer. "What's your mom's name again?"

"Cheryl Peterson."

I typed the name and then clicked on "images." About a million pictures came up on the screen.

"Whoa, we better narrow this down."

I typed "Cheryl Peterson, California." Then we heard a bump and a flush.

"Riley, we should get out of here."

"Not yet. Just lay down here. Even if someone opens the door they won't see us." We both got down between the side of the bed and the closet. I pointed to the pictures on the screen. "Okay, which one's your mom?"

"How am I supposed to know? Well, it's not that one, for sure." Rusty pointed to a picture of a toddler. "And probably not that one either." A senior citizen.

"Don't you remember anything about her at all?"

"Not much, except her eyes. They were bright. A light color. Blue or green."

"Which one?"

"Both eyes were the same color."

We both laughed a little too loud. Then we heard some stirring in the hallway.

"Girls? Hello?" Fawn's voice.

I motioned for Rusty to get down lower. I flattened myself on my stomach, and then realized that I had dug my newly painted toenails into the carpet. Rats. That would leave smudges.

Fawn knocked on a door, but it wasn't Flip's. It sounded like the door to Rusty's and my bedroom.

"Hey, anybody else awake and want a snack? I'm making popcorn."

When no one answered her, Fawn said, "Fine. The smell will wake you up."

Rusty stood up. "We better get outta here while she's in the kitchen."

I pulled her back down. "We've got a couple of minutes. Are you sure none of these ladies looks like your mom?"

Rusty pointed to a picture of a bodybuilder in a bikini. "What if it's *her*?"

I punched Rusty in the arm. "It's not."

"Riley, I don't feel right about—"

"Hey, let's email TJ and tell her what we're up to. She'll think it's cool."

"You're NOT going to use Flip's email."

"It'll be fine. I know TJ's email address by heart, and I'll delete it as soon as I send it. Flip will never see it."

I quickly typed up the email:

Hi TJ!

Rusty and I are looking for her long-lost mom on the Internet. We snuck in to Flip's room to use his computer. It's not as scary as when you, me, and Breanne snuck into his office, but it still feels like we're in a Nancy Drew mystery. I'll let you know how it all turns out.

But don't email me back, cuz—you know—it's Flip's email address!

Well, just wanted to say hi.

Love, Riley

Rusty read the email and then looked at me funny.

"Oops." I covered my face with my hands. "I shouldn't mention trying to find your mom, huh?"

Rusty thought a minute and then shrugged. "I guess it's okay for TJ to know. But don't tell any adults yet. I don't want them saying anything to my dad."

"Maybe TJ will have an idea of how we can find her."

I hit send. And then I smelled popcorn.

"Okay, can we get out of here now?" Rusty dug her fingers into my forearm.

"Yeah. Pretend like we just woke up. Don't forget to stretch and rub your eyes."

We escaped Flip's room undetected. I was careful to leave the door open halfway like we found it. We were just about to reach the kitchen when Rusty grabbed my arm again.

"What?"

"Did you delete the email?"

"Oh no! Go on into the kitchen and distract Fawn. I'll be right there."

I snuck back down the hall, keeping an eye out for Mom. I popped back behind the bed and reached for the keyboard to delete the email. I had to wait a minute though, since Flip had an email coming in.

"C'mon, you dumb machine." I tapped the side of the computer. "This is really bad timing."

I waited while the email downloaded. Fifty percent … seventy-five percent … one hundred percent. Finally.

I didn't mean to read it, but it was right in front of my face. From a guy named Drew Edwards. That name sounded familiar.

Dan,

Your brother's in trouble.

I don't know why I'm telling you this since I don't like either one of you.

I guess I just don't want your sister getting hurt. There might still be time if you talk to Eric.

Drew

I was stunned. My eyes kept going over and over the email, but it didn't make much sense. Who was Drew? And what kind of trouble was Eric in? And how was Fawn involved?

"Hey, who's popping popcorn? I want some!" I peeked up over the bed and saw Mom walking by Flip's room. Yikes. Time to delete the email and get out quick.

I highlighted it, clicked delete, and then I jumped up on my feet to run out the door. Somehow I managed to kick an opened book across the floor. The thing skidded all the way into the hallway. I reached out and pulled it back in, and was kinda surprised to see that it was a Bible. I checked the pages for toenail polish. Whew, none there. I straightened a couple of ruffled up pages and placed it back where I thought it had been, but there was no way to really know.

Now to act ... sleepy. Yawn.

By the time I got to the kitchen, the popcorn was almost gone. I grabbed the last handful and popped it in my mouth. It was mostly kernels, so I had to spit most of it back out so I wouldn't break my teeth. Fawn started a new batch for me in the air popper.

"Well, I guess that rafting really wore you out," Mom said. "I've never known you to take such a long nap." She pointed down at my feet. "What happened to your toes?"

Yikes. My pedicure. The cotton balls were still there, but the worse thing was all that carpet fuzz that was stuck to the polish on each toe.

Chapter 35

I couldn't sleep much that night. I was just getting comfortable with the thought that no bad guys were after us, and now this email made me wonder again. Worse yet was the fact that I couldn't tell anybody about it. Not Rusty, since she wasn't supposed to know about the whole Swiftriver "secret." Not Flip, because I was sneaking in his room. Not Mom. Wait ... *should* I tell Mom? Hmm. Definitely not Fawn. She'd been in such a good mood lately, probably because of Matt, and I didn't want to be the one to cause her to worry again.

My heart raced, and I had to wipe my sweaty palms on my pillow. Gross. After a couple of hours of staring at the ceiling, I found myself wishing for the new peace that Rusty seemed to have. But, I *was* supposed to have that peace, wasn't I? Mrs. O'Reilly, my teacher at church, who also happens to be Sean's mom, says that God's kind of peace is with you even when things are going wrong all around you. Well, things had definitely been going wrong lately. First, the Swiftriver nonsense. I sure got myself into a mess with that. Then, the Half Dome accident, which almost killed Flip. Images of that day still haunted my dreams. And now, just when I thought we had determined there were no bad people after us, this Drew guy shows up.

I rolled over to see Rusty sleeping, holding that locket in her hand.

God, where is Rusty's mom?

And then there was Sunday, and his leukemia coming back. I flipped over on my stomach and turned my pillow to the cool side. Burying my face in the pillow, I prayed as hard as I could:

Lord, please don't let Sunday die. Please ... please ... please ... please. I don't know what else to say. Please.

"Are you okay?" Rusty startled me.

My head shot up from the pillow.

"Huh? I guess so. Why?"

Rusty sat up in her bed and rubbed her eyes. "You were hitting the bed with your fist. Were you killing a spider?"

"What? Oh, sorry. No. I was praying for Sunday."

"Does punching make it a stronger prayer?"

"Um ... I dunno. I didn't realize I was doing it. Sorry I woke you up."

"It's okay. It's been fun sharing a room with you this week. Kinda like a never-ending slumber party. Too bad I have to go home."

"Yeah. Hey, you wanna go bake some cookies right now?"

Rusty looked over at the clock. "It's four o'clock!"

I flung off my covers. "They'll be done in time for breakfast."

"Okay." Rusty slid out of bed, shaking her head. "Let's go."

For the next few hours, we messed up the kitchen with flour, sugar, nuts, and chocolate. The aroma brought Flip and Brady out of their beds at five thirty.

"Girls are weird," Brady said, as he gobbled down a stack of warm chocolate chunk cookies. "Who else would make cookies for breakfast?"

"I can cook something else for you if you want," Flip said.

"No, thanks," Brady said. Yep, he's smart all right.

"Hey," Flip said, "Since we're up and filled with sugar, do you guys want to go for a morning ride in the ski boat?"

None of us had done that yet.

"Yeah!" Brady said. But then his smile changed to a frown. "But isn't that down by the lake?"

Flip seemed to know what that frown was all about. "It'll be okay. No bears this time, I promise."

That seemed to be enough for Brady. "I'll go get my jacket," he said. He took off toward our room. Rusty went to get hers too. I figured I might need one too, but as I got up to leave Flip caught me by the arm.

"Hold on there, squirt. We need to talk."

"We do?" I fidgeted and looked up at the ceiling.

"Yep. I know my room's a mess, but I also know when someone's been messing with my mess. If you wanted to use my computer, all you had to do was ask."

"Umm … sorry." When you're guilty, there's not much more you can say than that.

Brady yelled from the front entryway. "Are you guys coming?"

"On our way," Flip yelled back. He put his hands on his hips. "And WHAT did you do to my Bible?"

I cleared my throat and looked down. "I kicked it. I'm sorry."

Flip's mouth dropped open.

"I didn't mean to! I tried to run out of the room without getting caught and I didn't see it. Plus, why do you have a Bible in your room, anyway? Are you a Christian?"

Flip smiled. "Well … yeah." He threw his hands up in the air. "Okay, you got me. I'm a Jesus follower. Does that surprise you?"

I stared at him for a minute as I thought about that.

"I dunno. Maybe. You do a lot of good things, but you're pretty goofy. *And* when we first met, you told me that you didn't like church."

"That was my cover story. I couldn't go to church for a while or people might recognize me. *And* goofy people need forgiveness too."

"What about Fawn?"

"Fawn's not goofy at all."

I punched Flip in the arm. "Haha, you know what I mean. Is she a Christian too?"

Just then Brady charged into the kitchen. "Flip, can I drive the boat?"

"Uh, sure buddy. But first, I need to get your sister here to wrap my cast in some plastic bags so I don't get it wet. We'll meet you out front in just one minute."

Brady ran out, and Flip held up his stinky cast and wiggled his toes at me while I wrapped it in plastic.

"That's gross," I said.

"Yeah, well it's payback for kicking my Bible."

I finished wrapping his cast, and then we stared at each other. I wasn't going anywhere without an answer about Fawn.

Finally Flip spoke. "My sister is complicated. All I know is she used to come to church with our family all the time when she was a kid. Then one day—I think when she was about your age—she just stopped."

"Why?"

Flip shrugged. "Don't know. We've never talked about it."

"HEY!" Brady ran in again and pulled Flip off the barstool.

We walked out the door and toward the lake, and as Brady ran ahead to meet Rusty, Flip grabbed my arm one more time. "By the way," he whispered, "I saw that email, and I'll look into it. So you don't need to worry, okay? We'll figure it out, I promise."

I felt a weight lift off my shoulders.

Wow, thanks God. You sure took care of that Drew thing quickly!

Chapter 36

No bears showed up on our boat trip. We loved it so much, we begged Flip to take us out later in the day too. Fawn came with us and taught me how to wakeboard, which was really fun once I got the hang of it. I'm glad I hadn't had time to fix my pedicure yet, because shoving my feet into the boots on the board scratched my toenails up some more. And for some reason, I kept getting a cramp in my right foot, so bad that I screamed a little the second time, especially when I noticed my toes twisting out in all different directions.

Fawn reached into the water and grabbed my toes, pulling them up toward my shin.

"Ouch!" I yelled, but then the cramp faded away. "Oh, that's much better. That hurt just about worse than anything."

"Well, then, you haven't had much pain in your life, have you?"

Fawn was right, I hadn't. I wanted to keep it that way too.

"I wish I could try." If only Rusty could get her injured arm wet, I bet she would have been the best wakeboarder of all of us. I wondered if her dad would let her stay just a few more days so she could try. I decided I'd beg him when I saw him tomorrow.

Dinner that night was great. It was pot roast and mashed potatoes, with some veggies and rolls and strawberry shortcake for dessert. I still hadn't figured out who cooked all the food we'd been eating at the Stevens' resort.

"When's Sunday coming home?" Brady asked.

Flip rocketed a roll my direction since I asked for him to please pass the rolls. "Well, he may be home for a few days next week. But as soon as his bone marrow donor arrives, they're going to do the procedure."

"So he has a donor?" Mom asked.

"Yep, same one as last time. And she's still living in Montana. She's working at a Christian camp, so as soon as she finds a replacement, she'll be here."

"Does a bone marrow transplant hurt?" Brady asked.

Flip ignored Brady and asked for more dessert.

Ignoring Brady *never* works. "Flip, does it hurt?"

Dad broke in and saved Flip. "We'll look that up later, okay buddy? In the meantime, isn't it great that this young lady is a perfect match for Sunday? That's quite a miracle there."

"Yeah," my brother said. "And Flip's a miracle too, because he brought Sunday's family over here from Africa so they could get help."

The whole table got quiet, and all of a sudden I had trouble swallowing. Everyone stared at Flip, who blushed a little, then pushed himself back in his chair and hopped up on his good foot. "What does a guy have to do to get more dessert around here?"

"You know," Fawn said, "it's okay to accept a compliment once in a while." When Flip didn't respond, she picked up a roll and threw it in Flip's direction. He held up his hand to block the shot, and the roll ricocheted back and landed in the gravy, which splashed out on Fawn's pants.

"It figures." Fawn tried to wipe the gravy off her pants with a napkin, but it seemed to rub it in more. "No matter what I do, he always gets me back worse. What's up with brothers, anyway?"

Eric, on the other end of the table, chuckled. I looked over at him, and when our eyes met, he looked away and wiped his face with his napkin.

I really wanted to know what was up with that brother.

Chapter 37

I woke up before the sun on Friday morning. If I loved fishing, I suppose it would have been the perfect time to go. The thought of horrible fishing reminded me of Sunday, so I prayed for him again, this time without the pounding fist, so I wouldn't wake up Rusty.

God, please make it go away. Sunday's cancer, I mean. He's too young to have it. Not that anyone should have to have it. But why do people get cancer, anyway? I wish I understood a little more about how you do things.

Then I got a great idea. I grabbed my Bible and my headlamp off the nightstand.

I asked God to show me some answers. I had heard a lady talk in church once about how she asked God a question, then she opened her Bible, and it fell open to the verse that answered her question.

I decided to try it.

I held my Bible up and asked God to help me understand some things. Then I opened the Bible somewhere in the middle, closed my eyes and pointed to this verse:

"A person who doesn't want to work says, 'There's a lion in the road! There's an angry lion wandering in the streets!'" Proverbs 26:13

Hmm. What could that mean? I wished Mrs. O'Reilly were here to help me figure this strange verse out. Thinking of Mrs. O'Reilly reminded me of her son, Sean. I smiled and wondered if he was going to keep saving me chocolate donuts while I was gone. I felt a little sad and homesick, but I shook it off and got back to the Scripture about the lion. I slid out of bed and looked out the window. Thankfully, Montana has no lions. Well, maybe mountain lions—and bears.

I went back to my Bible. More verses about laziness. They were good to read, but they didn't answer my questions about Sunday's cancer. I guess the "open-the-Bible-and-point" method wasn't going to work for me like it did for that lady.

I decided to read the rest of the chapter since the verses were so interesting. If I remembered right, Mrs. O'Reilly taught us one time that King Solomon wrote the Proverbs, and he was supposed to be the wisest man that ever lived. I laughed out loud at the next verse:

"Don't get mixed up in someone else's fight as you are passing by. That's like picking a dog up by its ears." Proverbs 26:17

That reminded me that I hadn't begged my parents for a puppy in a while. Too busy with the shoe thing, I guess.

Focus, Riley. At least finish the chapter!

But I couldn't. But not because of lack of focus. It was because of the next to last verse:

"If anyone digs a pit, he will fall into it. If he rolls a big stone, it will roll back on him." Proverbs 26:27

And that reminded me of the Half Dome accident, when someone actually did roll some stones down on me and Flip. And then I got scared.

That's when a great big poofy "stone" came flying through the air and knocked my headlamp off my head and onto the floor.

"Hey!" I looked over at Rusty, who was now pillowless.

"Did I break it?" she asked.

I picked it up and flipped the switch. "Nah, it's okay."

She tossed her covers over her face. "Aww, that's too bad."

"I'm sorry. Was the light bothering you?"

"Not at first, when I thought it was the full moon. But when I figured out it was you, I couldn't control my pillow all of a sudden." She sat up and stretched. "What time is it, anyway?"

"I don't know."

"But you *do* know what day it is, right? You have the river shoot, and I'm flying back home today. I think we kind of need our sleep."

"Yeah."

"So can I have my pillow back?"

Rusty stood up and held her arms out. A perfect target.

"Sure, you can have it back."

That started a pillow war that lasted until the sun came up. We were so tired that we fell back asleep, missing breakfast totally. We might have slept all day if it weren't for the annoying pounding on our bedroom door.

"Girls! Do you know what time it is? I hope you're ready. We're leaving in twenty minutes."

We both popped our heads up.

"Leaving?" I yawned.

Mom opened the door and stepped inside, her eyes wide when she saw that we were still in bed. She placed her hand on her hip and just said two words:

"Ready Eddy."

Chapter 38

Fawn busted in right after Mom. "You're STILL in bed? You need to MOVE it, ladies! We've got shadows to beat!"

Then she ran out.

"What was that about shadows?" I asked Rusty.

Rusty had pulled her suitcase from the closet and was throwing all her clothes in. Oh yeah, she thought she was flying out after the shoot. I wished I could tell her not to bother, but sometimes surprises get tricky.

"Don't you remember at dinner last night, Flip said we had to be out on the rapids by noon so we don't end up with shadows in the photos."

"No, I don't remember that at all. I guess I really do need a personal assistant."

"Well, maybe since I'm helping him with the photography I was paying a little more attention than you were."

I jumped out of bed and pulled on my clothes. At least

I had the sense to get those ready the night before. And the Ready Eddy sandals were a no-brainer. I brushed my fingers through my tangled waves. Great. Fawn was going to have to do something about those on the way to the river. Or maybe no one would care since I'd be wearing a helmet.

Chapter 39

Fawn dragged the comb through the last of my snarls before we climbed into the SUV.

"Ouch! Is this really necessary? I'm wearing a helmet, right?"

"Yes, but we're taking some pictures before you get in the raft. We want you to look good before you turn into a drowned rat."

"After that happens, we'll focus on the shoes," Flip said. "I can't believe I'm asking this, but did you redo your pedicure?"

I stuck my beautiful toes up near his face.

"Riley, don't be gross," Mom said.

Flip laughed. "I had that one coming, Mrs. Hart."

We all jumped into the SUV and Fawn drove.

"Where are all the other guys?" I asked. "We're not doing this alone, are we?"

"Matt took your Dad, Brady, and Chuck up there early so they could help him take the raft off the van and carry it down to the river," Fawn said. "He was thinking it would be nice not to get squashed this time around."

"And we can't have our spokesgirl getting dusty and beat up," Flip added.

"Wow, it's like you're a star or something," Rusty said.

Mom handed me a magazine over the front seat. "Have you seen this yet?"

It was the latest copy of Outdoor Teen Magazine. And there I was, featured in the main article, climbing up Half Dome. The article was titled Girl vs. Rock. And the writer was Nate Johnson. I had sort of forgotten about him since we left him and Matt to climb back down the mountain when we left in the helicopter. When Fawn turned hysterical after Flip's accident, she had warned Nate not to write about it in the article. I skimmed it, and from what I could tell, the story was just about me, the climb, and of course, my Rock Shocker hiking boots.

"These pictures are great, Flip. I look like I'm really enjoying myself."

"Well, you did, right?" Flip turned around, looked at Rusty, and winked at me.

I smiled. "One of the most exciting experiences ever."

"Until today," Fawn said.

Fawn pulled off the paved road, and we bumped along the side of the river until we reached the van and the men. The raft was in the water already, and life vests and paddles were neatly organized on a tarp on the ground. A table with fruit, crackers, cheese, and a variety of drinks was set up under a big canopy. Beach chairs lined the edge of the river.

"Where did this stuff come from?" I asked.

"We men set it up for you," Brady said. He looked to me like he had grown an inch or so.

I grabbed a bunch of grapes off the table and popped one in my mouth. "I like this way better than the dress rehearsal."

"Don't get too comfortable over there in the shade. We need pictures of those gleaming sandals." Flip motioned for me to come over to the raft. Then he took several photos of me putting on my life vest, pretending to pack supplies, and sitting on the front of the raft kicking up water with my feet. That was my favorite pose. Flip showed me the digital picture, and it was amazing how he managed to catch the sun shining off the gold nuggets on the sandals, surrounded by a circular pattern of water droplets.

The shoe spokesgirl thing could sure be fun—at times.

"Okay, ladies, party's over. We need to shove off and hit some waterfalls." Matt sat on the back of the raft, looking much less dusty than the last time around. "Let me check those vests before we go."

"Mine still smells like fish," I said.

Matt adjusted the straps. "Yeah, but you'll appreciate

having it on if you fall in the water. Do you remember what to do if that happens?"

Mom and Fawn were now standing by my side all suited up in their vests. They stared at me.

"What, is this a test?"

"Yes," Matt said. Then he stared at me too.

I panicked a minute. What *was* I supposed to do if I fell in? "Do you guys all remember what to do?"

"Yes," they said.

"Oh. Okay. Just checking. Hmm, if I fall out ..." I looked around and noticed Flip and Rusty slinging photography gear over their shoulders. "If I fall out, I keep my head above water and smile real big for the camera?"

"Yes—but no," Fawn said.

Matt crossed his arms and gave me the stink-eye. "If you fall out, lay on your back like you're in a lounge chair with your feet in front of you. If you're in a waterfall, hold your breath and curl up in a ball until you pop up. Then swim for the eddy."

"Remember—go against the flow," Fawn said.

"Oh yeah, that's right. I guess the reason I didn't remember is because I don't plan to fall out. I'm the raft pancake, remember?"

"And soon you will be a soggy one," Matt said.

Chapter 40

Flip and Rusty were going to have the hardest job during this shoot. Their goal was to get pictures at every rapid, but they were going to have to travel by foot down the side of the river. At first, Flip had thought about traveling in a raft in front of us, which would have made it easier, but he still had that cast, which he couldn't get wet. But after some good scouting during our practice run, he was able to find some really good views from land. He was just going to have to struggle to get there quickly.

Flip yelled to us and waved as he and Rusty took off down the trail. "The best shots are going to be from Butter-Churn and Get-Out-Now, so save some smiles for the end!"

As Matt ran over to get our paddles, Fawn grabbed me and Mom. "I'd really like to shake our guide up a little on the Morning Coffee rapid. Are you game?"

Of course we were game. So we hatched a plan.

Matt broke up our little huddle. "Ladies, we're going to change things up a bit with the seating. We need Riley in the front right, and Fawn in the front left. Mrs. Hart, you can sit behind Riley, and I'll just move wherever I'm needed."

"But the front is where all the waves hit," I said.

"Exactly," Matt said. "That's how Flip wanted it."

"Great. I'll get him back later."

"Be careful," Fawn said. "He always gets you back worse." I laughed, remembering Fawn's gravy pants.

Matt lifted me into the raft and before I knew it, we were shoved off and reviewing the rafting commands. Only this time I was on the other side, so I really had to think.

"All forward into Morning Coffee!" Matt yelled.

Fawn began counting loud. "One, two … three!"

As we entered the rapid, all of us women stood up. We raised our paddles in the air and gave a big "Whoop!"

The cold wave of water hit us hard. It stung my legs and arms and neck, and it felt like I had done a belly flop in a pool. A ways down on the bank, I could see Flip snapping pictures and Rusty cheering us on. The Class One rapid didn't last long. I waited for Matt's reaction. I expected another stink eye or a firm warning, but instead, he grabbed his stomach, laughed, and shook his head. "Wow—I thought you were all flying out there!"

"Gotcha," Fawn said.

"Yeah, well just remember, pride goeth before a fall."

"We were just having a little fun. We'll be good now. Promise." Fawn looked over at me and winked.

The next rapid was Break Neck, the one that turns you into a human bobblehead. Fawn thought it would be funny to have us act like we were drinking tea out of pretend cups—pinkies up and everything—while Matt pushed us from behind. It made for another great picture if Rusty's reaction from the shore meant anything. As soon as Flip took a few shots, we dug our paddles into the shallow river to help Matt dislodge us from the rocks. This time he was able to jump in without any drama.

"I thought this *wasn't* a tea party," he said.

"Yeah, well, we changed our minds," Fawn said.

That made me laugh, but just for a minute. In the distance, I could hear the churning and whooshing sounds of our first waterfall. My stomach did a little jump, but this time, I knew the feeling wouldn't go away until we had successfully made it down the Tube Chute.

My ears started to pound, or I guess maybe that was just me hearing my heart kick up a notch. Our last attempt through the Tube Chute was botched when we hit that rock and got stuck on it. All I could think about was that I couldn't remember what to do if it happened again. Matt didn't review that with us.

Matt yelled from the back of the raft. "Left forward, right back!"

We did as we were told. But what we did couldn't be right. We started spinning in circles. The churning water sound got louder.

"Matt! What are you doing?" Fawn's eyes were wide as she watched the rock getting closer and closer.

"I'm paying you back!" Matt yelled. "Now, all forward—HARD!"

As soon as we dug our paddles in, the raft straightened out.

"GET DOWN!" We all held our paddles as we flattened out on the bottom of the raft. I watched as we flew by the rock. I threw my hands up in a victory pose—just in time to plunge down the waterfall. In all the excitement, I forgot to hold my breath before we went under. I *did* remember to smile when we came back up, but I'm not sure how that picture turned out, because the water that had filled up my mouth squirted out of my teeth.

"That was THRILLING, wasn't it?" Matt stood up and gave us all high fives as the waters calmed a bit.

Mom shook herself like a dog when it's done with its bath. "Hey, Bucko, what was with the spinning?"

"Sorry, Mrs. Hart. I had it under control the whole time. You can thank Fawn for your little adventure."

"I'm sorry," Fawn said. "But we're even now, right?"

Matt blushed a little. "Yeah, we're even. But if the tea

party's not over yet, this would be a good time to get out some dinner rolls. Butter-Churn is next."

I tried to remember about Butter-Churn. "Is this a waterfall, Matt?"

"A small one. The rapid is a little rough. The river narrows, and then we have to weave through rocks on both sides. You'll all paddle forward and put on a show for Flip, and I'll do the tricky maneuvering back here. After that is Get-Out-Now, and then we can have cookies and relax, because we're definitely not going down Thrill-and-Kill today."

"Only two more waterfalls. Easy as pie."

I'm not sure why Fawn used that term. I've tried to make pie before and it wasn't easy. The crust shrank and then burned, and the filling bubbled out all over the inside of the oven which caused smoke to fill the kitchen. When things are going to be easy, I don't say that they're easy as pie. I always say they're "cake."

Chapter 41

The river ran smooth for a few minutes, giving us time to ham it up a little for the camera. Flip was a ways down the embankment, but had these enormous camera lenses that help him photograph things from miles away. So we smiled and waved, and then we actually did "The Wave." We spelled "hi" with our paddles, but I was giggling so much I had to sit down, so then it looked like "li." We almost distracted Flip too much. I saw Rusty tug on his shirt and point down the river. Then he gave us a quick wave and hobbled out of sight. I watched a minute to see if they made it to the top of the lookout beyond the Butter-Churn rapids, but I didn't see them before we had to get our game faces on and start paddling.

I heard the rushing water again, only this time my ears didn't pound so much. I was glad because it made it easier to hear Matt's commands.

"Okay ladies, a rapid and two waterfalls, right in a row. Let's finish this thing! ALL FORWARD."

I felt extra strong this time. I shoved my foot under the seat in the raft to secure myself. The river narrowed up in front of us, and I dug my paddle in the water as hard as I could. I watched as we approached the first tall, flat rock of the Butter-Churn. Then I remembered how this rapid went from practice. Three big rocks that look like paddles in a butter churn. We just needed to make sure we didn't hit any of them.

"Get down!" I guess Matt didn't need our help any further. I brought my paddle up and got ready for the plunge.

Right before I flattened out on the bottom of the raft, I noticed something moving in the water in front of us. It looked like a big bunch of branches or something. No worries. Our raft would run right over whatever it was. At least that's what I thought. Instead, whatever it was rose out of the water, caught my paddle and yanked it right out of my hand.

"AAAAAHHHHH!" I heard Matt yell. Then I heard nothing. I was afraid my paddle had hit him in the head. I looked back, praying he wouldn't be sitting there with a bloody forehead.

But he wasn't sitting there at all. Matt was gone.

Rock number two was approaching so fast that we didn't have time to do anything to avoid it. So we hit.

The force from the river pushed the back of the raft around so that we were now riding backwards, headed straight for rock number three.

"Brace yourself!" Mom launched herself on top of me and grabbed a handle on the side of the raft. "Hold on, Riley," she cried as we hit rock number three—hard. Then we stuck there.

"Tube suck!" Fawn shouted. "High side!" She grabbed Mom and pulled her up to the back of the raft. I stayed plastered to the floor as I watched them struggle to bounce the raft off the rock. But the current was too strong—the water had us pinned. They needed more weight to free the raft. Just a few more pounds. They needed ... me.

The next seconds seemed like slow motion. Staying in a crouched position, I turned to face the back of the raft. I crawled—grabbing hold of the side handles—up to where I could reach Mom's feet. "Pull me up!" I held my hand up to Mom.

She shook her head at first, but then the front of the raft started taking on water. It curled under us from the force of the river. We were going to flip! Mom grabbed my hand and pulled me up. I stood and bounced with everything I had, which broke the suction of the water and released our raft—front first—right at the top of the waterfall.

The next thing I knew, I was in the river, over my

head. The water swirled above and below me, and I felt around, hoping that the raft was somewhere nearby. I couldn't see anything. I tried to swim, but the current was so strong it was no use.

Turn on your back. Like a lounge chair.

I somehow remembered Matt's words and managed to flip over on my back. My feet bounced off rocks, but I was finally able to look up and see the sun. I gulped for air and turned my head in every direction looking for the raft. I finally saw it—behind me.

Someone yelled "Hang on, Riley," but what was I supposed to hang on to? Branches hung low over the edges of the river. If I could just swim to one, maybe I could grab it. I tried once and missed. On the second try I got one. But the river's pull was too strong, and it yanked me back in the water.

That's when I smashed the back of my hand on something hard. Rock number four. I'd forgotten about that one.

The pain in my hand was unbearable for a second, but then, when the whole thing went numb, I was sure it had been ripped from my body. I grabbed for it with my other hand, and pulled it up to my face to make sure it was still there. Whew, yes, there it was. I thought of softball for a brief moment, and about the importance of having both hands to play. Whatever was wrong could be fixed—I hoped—as long as it was still attached. But for now, I was going to swim like crazy with just the left hand.

Chapter 41

"RILEY!" Mom screamed, and I looked back again to see her point forward and then wrap her arms around her body. She looked like she was curling up into a ball.

That's when I realized what I was supposed to do next. Ball up. Because it was time for GET-OUT-NOW.

Chapter 42

Going down the eight-foot waterfall in the raft during practice had been fun and smooth. This time—with just my body—was horrifying. When I plunged over the top, it was like I was doing a cannonball off the high dive at the city pool. I grabbed my knees and rolled into a tight little ball. My stomach lurched, and I held my breath, expecting to go under at the bottom. I did, but then I didn't come up right away, like I do at the city pool. Instead, I hit bottom and stayed there, an invisible weight holding me down. I choked a little, kicked my feet and struggled with all my might to free myself. It was no use. I was running out of time and air. I screamed for help with my mouth closed and realized that my feet, and my Ready Eddy river sandals, were buried in the bottom of the river. I imagined what the next magazine article would say:

. . . and that was the end of that Riley Mae shoe-girl.

NO! I couldn't let that happen. I had a two-year contract, after all, and I wasn't allowed to break it!

Suddenly, I realized that I wasn't in a ball anymore and that I needed to be. NOW. I pulled my feet out of the mud and grabbed my knees, prayed, and waited. For light. For air. For life.

And then I popped back up. Like a ping-pong ball.

But I barely had time to celebrate, because as soon as I got to the surface, I remembered that the Thrill-and-Kill was next. And that was a waterfall I wouldn't survive.

"MOM! Where are you?" I turned in a full circle as the water propelled me farther down the river. I spotted the raft, now in front of me, pulled out of the water on my right side. Fawn was standing, holding a rope, in a pool of water that looked like it swirled up river. The eddy.

Go against the flow, Riley.

That's what I intended to do.

"Swim hard," Fawn yelled. "I'm going to throw the rope!"

I tried to move my arms, but the only one that cooperated was the one that didn't have the smashed hand. I kicked my feet, and for a minute I think I was able to stay in one place in the river. But the fighting was exhausting, and soon I was being pulled close to the Thrill-and-Kill rapids. I heard Mom scream my name again, and I closed my eyes, not believing that everything was really going to end this way.

Chapter 43

And then I couldn't breathe. But it wasn't because I was drowning. It was because someone was holding me around the neck really tight.

"Relax girl, I gotcha." Matt was in the water next to me. And he was swimming toward the eddy with all his might—with one hand.

I pulled his arm away from my neck a little. "I thought I killed you with my paddle."

He didn't say anything until later, after we were both safely on shore. "Your paddle? Is that what knocked me out of the raft?"

"I'm not sure, but something pulled it out of my hand." I stretched out my right hand and cringed when I saw the blown-up looking thing. I still couldn't feel it either.

Mom ran over, picked me up, and carried me over to a beach chair. She wrapped some towels around me and rubbed my arms and back to warm me up. Fawn ran over with a sports drink, but I didn't feel like drinking it.

"Where's Dad and Brady?" I couldn't think of a time when I wanted to have my whole family together more than right then.

"They went to pick Rusty's dad up from the airport," Mom said. Then she started to cry—which Mom hardly ever does. "I was afraid I was going to have to tell them that we lost you."

"Nah," Matt said. "I wasn't going to let that happen. Are you okay, Riley? Besides your hand, I mean." He rested my hand in his and lightly pressed on the huge knob that had grown on the back of it.

"Owwww."

"Sorry. I'm afraid our next stop is the ER."

"For both of you." Fawn pointed to a huge gash on Matt's right knee.

Great. More hospitals.

Matt put pressure on the knee with a towel and shook his head. "I got this from rock number two. But I still can't figure out what hit me and pulled me out of the raft. I'm sure it wasn't a paddle. But whatever it was caused these."

He pointed to a bunch of little welts on his face and upper body.

Fawn inspected them from close up. "They look like rope burns."

"Hey," I said, "I saw something strange looking in the

water, just before my paddle flew out of my hands. It looked like branches, but it could have been a rope."

Mom went into cop mode. "What would a rope be doing in the river?"

"Maybe a rope swing came loose from one of the trees," Fawn said.

"But we would have ridden right over it," Matt said. "No, whatever it was, I got caught up in it."

"Like a net." Mom said. "Maybe you ran into a fisherman."

"Fishing for what?" I asked. "A whale?"

"Something even bigger. Revenge, maybe?" Mom raised her eyebrows and looked at Fawn.

Fawn shook her head. "No! Nobody knows where we are. You said yourself that we were probably out of danger."

"Yes, I did say *probably*. Nothing's for sure yet."

Matt put an arm around Fawn. "So you think this was intentional? Someone actually tried to hurt us out there?"

"Maybe," Mom said. She looked up into the mountains. "And if that's the case, they could be watching us. We need to pack up and get out of here right now."

I groaned a little. My hand was starting to warm up, and with that came some pretty sharp pain.

"Hey! Riley Mae Hart! You never told me you were a stunt woman!" Flip came jog-limping down the hill from the photography lookout. Rusty dragged behind him, carrying most of the equipment. "I got some gnarly shots of Matt doing the backward flip off the raft and then you—not to be outdone—cranking out that awesome cannonball off the Get-Out-Now. I can't wait to check out the frame-by-frame!"

Rusty dropped the equipment and kneeled down next to my chair. "Are you okay? That looked terrifying."

I showed her my hand. She grabbed her stomach and made a horrible face.

Flip saw it too. "Oh no. You weren't supposed to get hurt. I'm sorry, kiddo." He looked up and saw Matt's knee, which was bleeding pretty good. "And you—I thought you were made of steel."

Matt laughed. "It's not as bad as it looks. A couple of stitches and I'll be ready to go again."

"Flip, did you say you had frame-by-frame shots?" Mom was frantically folding up chairs and towels. Chuck, who had driven down to meet us at the pull-out, offered to carry me over to the car. "I'll get you to the doc right quick, and we'll get that hand fixed up good as new."

"Just don't go too quick," I said. "And I could use another Samantha Special."

"Sure thing, little darlin'. You've been through more bumps on this trip than a bull-ridin' cowboy. Maybe you should join the rodeo. You're tougher 'n nails, from what I can gather."

The rodeo. That might be interesting. I could imagine wearing some sparkly Riley Mae cowboy boots and laying in a hospital bed with a matching neck collar.

But for now, it would probably be a cast or something on my right hand.

Chapter 44

We didn't go straight to the emergency room. I had forgotten that Rusty was supposed to fly home. Or at least that we were going to pretend to send her on her way.

"Drop us off at our place, and Eric and I can take Rusty to the airport," Fawn said.

"I wish you were coming too," Rusty said to me.

I tried to look disappointed. "Me too. I should be back home in Fresno soon though. They can't really make me work too much with this messed-up hand."

"I hope it's not broken."

I tried to make a fist with it, but my fingers wouldn't move. "I think it is."

"That's your throwing hand."

"Thankfully the season's over."

Flip leaned over the back seat and cut into our conversation. "Man, practically everyone in this car is on the disabled list."

We dropped Rusty and Fawn off at the Stevens' resort. Everyone hugged Rusty and said good-bye like they weren't going to see her for a long time. Dad and Brady had to be back from the airport with her dad by now. I wished I could go in and watch Rusty's reaction, but Chuck squealed the tires and tore out toward the hospital before I got a chance to ask if I could.

The ride to the hospital was short, as is every car ride with Chuck. I think I sort of fell asleep, because even though I felt like talking, my mouth wouldn't work. I could hear Matt telling Chuck about what happened on the river, and I tried to force myself to dream about something else. I think for a minute I dreamed about those sparkly cowboy boots, but then my throbbing hand woke me up.

"We're here!" Chuck pulled right up to the entrance of the ER. "I wonder if Diane's workin'." He opened the door and pulled me out and carried me in like a little baby. How embarrassing. I was still wrapped up in my towels from the river. Moving from the warm car to the cool emergency room gave me the shivers.

Matt and Mom went to check in while Flip and Chuck sat next to me on a cushy bench. I couldn't stop my teeth from chattering.

"You poor little thing! I'm gonna go find you a blanket." Chuck clomped off in his nonsparkly cowboy boots.

Flip moved over and sat next to me. He had his camera with him, and he was fiddling with it.

"What are you doing?" I asked.

"Investigating."

"You sound like my mom."

"You want to see your cannonball?"

"Sure."

Flip handed me the camera. The display on the back showed a close-up of my face as I cannonballed down the Get-Out-Now waterfall.

"My mouth's wide open. That's attractive."

"I think it's an amazing shot," Flip said. "Too bad we can't use it."

"Why not?"

"The shoes aren't in focus."

"Oh that's right. It's *all* about the shoes."

He smiled and elbowed me. "Well, it kinda is."

He grabbed the camera back and clicked to another picture. "Now *this* one we'll use."

It was a picture of the tube suck. When I was climbing up the back of the raft to try to bounce it off rock number three. Somehow, Flip got a close-up of just me, stretching upward to grab Mom's hand, with the bottom of one of the shoes showing off the Riley Mae logo.

"That's a crazy picture," I said.

"I know. You have an awesome genius for a photographer."

Matt and Mom seemed to have disappeared forever. And where was Chuck with that blanket? I continued to chatter away on my teeth as Flip clicked through the pictures.

"How many pictures did you take, anyway?"

Flip didn't answer.

"Flip?"

Nothing.

I looked over at him. His mouth was hanging open.

"Are you okay?" He still didn't answer.

Just then, Chuck came around the corner with a big fuzzy blue blanket—and nurse Diane. "Check it out, I found the best two things in this here hospital."

Flip looked up from his camera. "And I think I just found our volleyball net."

Chapter 45

"Riley Mae Hart?" A pretty, but tired-looking nurse stepped through the double automatic doors. She stood with her hand on her hip and held a folder in her hand as she scanned the beat-up crowd in the ER.

"Um ... here," I said. I tried to raise my hand, but it hurt, so I just stood up. When I did, Diane grabbed the damp towels off of me and replaced them with the blanket. She put her arm around me and led me toward the nurse with the folder. "I've got this one, Kelli."

Kelli looked disappointed. "Are you sure? I'd really like to work on a nice little girl. I've been with grouchy patients all morning."

Diane smiled and winked. "If you go give Elizabeth her break, you can take her patient. A real handsome hunk with a knee that needs stitching up."

"Thanks for the tip," Kelli said. She turned around and skipped back through the automatic doors.

So Matt was already checked in. Where was Mom?

Diane led me to an empty half room, sat me down on a bed, and drew a curtain around me. She handed me a little piece of cloth and told me to change out of my wet clothes, and she'd be back in a minute with Mom.

She disappeared too quickly for me to ask what I was supposed to wear after I took my clothes off. I guessed that the cloth was for drying myself, so after I managed to peel my clothes off with one hand, I opened up the cloth and started to wipe my legs. That was when I noticed that it wasn't just a little cloth. It was a dress, or . . . something. It did have a couple of arm holes, but it only had one side. And strings hung off the back. Or maybe that was the front. Yes, it was half a dress. WHAT was I supposed to do with *that*?

People kept walking by and brushing the thin curtains that separated them from naked me. I had to cover up—and quick. I decided that *if* I had to expose a side of myself to the world, it would have to be the backside. So, I put my arms through the sleeves with the half dress covering my front. I guessed the strings were for tying it on, but I couldn't do it with my blown-up hand. I grabbed the blanket and wrapped it around my backside, and I tried to hop up on the bed. Unfortunately, with just one good hand to hold the blanket up, I only got a part of it under my legs. The rest of it hung down to the floor.

Diane and a young man walked in, and I felt my face

heat up. I raised my shoulders, hoping the dress would stay on.

"Hi Riley, I'm Doctor Harris. I hear you had a little collision with a rock."

Diane walked behind me and tied my strings. "There," she said. "Is that better?"

"Sure, except for the missing back."

The doctor laughed. "Yeah, the hospital really needs to put more into the clothing budget." He opened a drawer and handed another folded-up cloth to Diane. "I think we can afford to give her the other half."

Diane draped the new gown around my back and helped me put my arms through the sleeves.

Okay, now I could relax … a little.

Doctor Harris examined my hand by poking and twisting my wrist all around. The twisting didn't hurt, but the poking sure did.

"I'm pretty sure you broke some bones here." He pointed to the top of my hand. "But it doesn't look bad enough to need surgery. We'll do some X-rays to confirm, but my prediction is that you'll be leaving here today in a cast. The good news is you can pick the color."

"Orange," I said.

The doctor raised his eyebrows. "Orange, huh? Most girls pick pink or purple."

Diane smiled at me. "Orange is perfect."

"Okay." Doctor Harris scribbled something on a file.

"I'll see you back here in a little while and I'll try to dig up some orange bandages."

Mom *finally* arrived from somewhere. "Sorry, Honey. I had to get all your paperwork filled out, and then I had some phone calls to make. Your dad and Brady send their love. Rusty says hi. She's thrilled that her dad came to visit." She patted me on the knee and lifted my hand to look at it, then turned to Diane.

"How's our patient, nurse?"

Diane seemed a little distracted reading my file.

"Diane? What did the doctor say?"

"Oh, were you talking to me? I'm sorry. The doc says it needs a cast. But first, X-rays."

"Oh my. I guess you really crunched it." Mom reached over and gave me a hug. She was still in her wet river clothes.

"How's Matt?" I asked.

"He's getting stitches," Diane said. "But he's in good hands with Nurse Kelli."

"Fawn won't like that."

Diane took a little brown bottle out of a drawer.

"Uh-oh," I pulled the front of my dress over my skinned-up knees. "I've seen that before."

"Yes, I'm sorry, but you've got some scrapes here on your legs and arms that I need to disinfect."

I yelped a little while Diane scrubbed me up.

"You must think I don't take very good care of my

kids," Mom said. "We don't usually go to the ER this much."

Diane shrugged. "No worries. Things happen, especially in the great outdoors. Kids are not easy to keep track of all the time."

"Do you have kids?" I asked Diane.

Mom glared at me, like I had burped out loud or something.

Diane was quiet for a moment as she wiped one of my scrapes with the cotton ball. "Yes, actually. I have a daughter." She popped the trash can lid with her foot and tossed the cotton ball in. "But she doesn't live with me right now."

"Has she ever broken a bone?" I cringed as Diane soaked another cotton ball with disinfectant and rubbed it on my elbow.

"I don't know. I sure hope not."

"Why don't you know?" This time, Mom gave me her famous "zip-your-lip" stare.

Before Diane could answer my question, a man with a squeaky rolling table barged through the curtain. "I'm looking for a Riley Mae Hart." He flipped through a file. "Let's see ... broken hand." He looked at mine, and his eyes got big. "Must be you! Ready to go for a ride?"

"On that? Can't I walk? My foot's not broken."

He shook his head. "Afraid not. The ride's part of the deal. But the squeaks will cost you extra." He reached over and lifted me from the soft bed to the table. "Oh, I see they upgraded you to the superdeluxe gown. I wouldn't want to pay *your* bill."

So off I went with the jokester table driver. I ended up in the X-ray room—all by myself again. Mom had mentioned something about making another phone call as I squeaked off.

Mom and her phone calls.

Chapter 46

My brother Brady seemed way too excited about my broken hand. He ran outside to meet me when we arrived back at the Stevens' resort, and then he guided me inside the main lodge where the gang was all waiting. "Wow, wait till Sunday sees your orange cast! Dad, can we drive down there tomorrow and show him?"

"I don't know, Buddy. Riley needs her rest. She's pretty scraped up, and I'm sure her hand really hurts." Dad knelt down and gave me a long hug.

"Nah, I'm good," I said. "I want to go see him." The truth was that my hand throbbed, and I was exhausted. But I really wanted to see Sunday before his bone marrow transplant.

"We could all go," Rusty said. "Now that I'm staying for a couple more days." She was all smiles. "You keep a good secret." She gave me a hug.

"It's a two-hour drive to Missoula," Mom said. "Are you sure you're up for that?"

"I think it will be a lot easier than going down a waterfall without a raft."

"Yeah, that was a burly ride," Flip said. "Nice cast, though. It matches the Sole Fire."

"The what?"

"The orange running shoe—Sunday's favorite. It's been one of our top sellers, so we gave it a cooler name, and we're making it the focus of our next marketing campaign. Good thing only your hand's hurt. It'd be hard to train for a 5K if you had a broken foot."

"A five what?"

Flip ignored me and turned his attention to my mom. "Mrs. Hart, I need to talk to you ASAP. Got something to show you." Then they both took off somewhere. Flip had his camera. Great. He was probably going to show her that crazy cannonball picture.

Matt limped over with Fawn to check out my cast. "I'm sorry I wasn't there to protect you from that rock."

"That's okay," I said. "You saved me from the Thrill-and-Kill. How's your knee?"

He pulled off the big bandage to show me. "Eight stitches."

"That's gonna leave a mark," I said.

"Yep. I could tell you my life story by my scars."

"Most people do that through scrapbooking," Fawn said.

We all laughed.

"We *could* scrapbook it," I said. "Wait till you see some of the pictures Flip took."

"Maybe we could get him to put together a slide show for after dinner tonight," Fawn said.

Dinner. The mention of it made my mouth water. The last thing I remember eating was a Tylenol at the hospital. Before that, all I could remember was sucking water out of the river.

Matt must have read my mind. "Right now I need to eat a predinner dinner. You think there's any meat in the kitchen?"

I followed Matt on the hunt for food. I never thought a roast beef sandwich could taste so good. Or potato salad. But the pickle to top it all off was the best.

"This is the most delicious predinner dinner I've ever had." It was actually the only one I had ever had.

Matt laughed as he piled the beef on his second sandwich. "I don't know about you, but riding the rapids without a raft makes me hungry."

Flip crashed through the double-doors leading into the kitchen. "Has anybody seen Eric?"

"Eric?" I had to think. Last time I had seen him was dinner the night before.

"Not since we've been home," Matt said. "Come to think of it, he never showed up to help us with the raft this morning."

Fawn crashed through the doors next. "His room is empty!"

"What do you mean?" Flip said.

"His stuff is gone. He's gone."

Another crash. Mom this time.

"We've got more trouble. I finally got through to Tyler. Seems Eric lied to us about the plane."

Matt looked as confused as I was. "Are you talking about the landing gear malfunction?"

"Yep. Someone tampered with it," Mom said. "Tyler confirmed it."

Flip shook his head. "But Eric said that Tyler said—"

"Eric lied," Mom said.

"Why would he do that?" Fawn asked.

"That's a good question," Mom said. "Too bad he's not here to answer it."

Fawn paced back and forth in the little space between Matt's and my sandwiches. "There has to be a good explanation for him being gone."

"There is," Flip said, "but you're not going to like it."

Fawn stopped pacing and stared intently at Flip. "NO. *Don't* say it. He's our brother! I won't believe it."

"Then I won't say a thing. I'll just let you see for yourself." Flip placed his camera in Fawn's hands. She plunked down on the barstool and pressed her fingers into her forehead.

Mom grabbed the camera from Fawn. "Flip, can you

put these pictures on a CD? We need to see them on a bigger screen."

"Sure. Meet me in the game room in ten minutes."

Fawn cried as Flip picked up the camera and limped out of the room.

Chapter 47

The "special picture viewing" was attended by all except Brady, Rusty, and her dad. I wished I was with them doing whatever they were doing, because I had a feeling that things were about to get sticky—like when you leave a soda can in the freezer too long and it pops.

Flip inserted the picture CD in the player, and we all grabbed seats on the couches that surrounded the big-screen TV in the game room. Flip sat on the floor in front of us, and he used the remote to skip past all the fun pictures on Morning Coffee and Break Neck. He went right to the mess at the Butter-Churn.

"I'm going to advance slowly through these pictures," he said. "About the fifth one in is when it happens ..."

"What happens?" I asked.

"Shh." Mom placed her hand on my shoulder.

I watched as our raft approached the rapids. That was good. Rock number one came into view. Still good. Then

I saw that weird looking thing in the water. Okay. Next frame was when we all obeyed Matt's command to get down. And we did.

But that's why we didn't see what happened next. As soon as we hit the floor of the raft, a net—and upon closer examination, we saw that it was a *volleyball net*—rose up out of the water and tore the paddle out of my hands. It somehow missed Mom's and Fawn's paddles, but it sure didn't miss Matt's shoulders and head. Since he was still sitting on the back ledge of the raft, it caught him and pulled him out.

"No wonder you have welts," Fawn said.

"Keep watching," Flip crawled up closer to the TV.

The next frame showed Matt basically doing a back flip out of the raft.

"Nice," Matt said. "Next is when I hit the rock with my knee."

"Not quite yet," Flip said. "First we catch the net holders—or at least one of them."

Sure enough, as the frame-by-frame followed Matt downriver, it also caught a man on the riverbank holding the end of the net.

Flip paused the slide show. "There. We have our villain."

I squinted at the blur-of-a-person. "He's so small."

"That's why I enlarged it. Check this out." Flip clicked to the next frame.

It was definitely someone I'd seen before.

"That's not Eric," Matt said.

"No." Fawn jumped up off the couch. "That's Drew!"

"Okay, so who's Drew?" Matt asked.

I didn't know, exactly. But I *had* seen an email from him on Flip's computer. And if this picture was of Drew, then he was also the guy who had been arguing with Eric before he took off in the Jeep with all my leftover cookies.

"Drew Edwards is Chuck's son," Fawn said.

"Lucky Chuck?" I squirmed in my seat and shot a glance toward Flip. Would he tell about the email?

But Flip didn't change expression at all. "Eric told me he was back."

"Back? From where?" Mom jotted down notes in her fancy police folder.

"If it's Drew, it's not from anywhere good," Flip said.

"Why didn't you tell me?" Fawn asked.

Flip shrugged. "We've been kind of busy around here. Plus, I haven't heard from him or seen him at all."

I raised my eyebrows and looked at Flip.

What about the email?

He looked back at me. "What's that look for, shoe-girl?"

Oh no. I cleared my throat. Here's where the soda can exploded.

"Um ... well, I was wondering. Maybe Drew called someone. Or texted. Maybe an email? Just ... thinking."

"And why would you think such a thing?" Mom had her hand on her hip. Rats, she already knew something was up. Might as well spill it.

Everyone in the room was now staring at me. I started to cry a little.

"It's okay, Honey," Dad said. "Just tell us what you know."

Now my head throbbed harder than my hand.

"Okay, this is what happened. I snuck into Flip's room to use his computer for ... something ..."

I looked around. No one freaked out yet.

"... and while I was using it, an email came in."

"Go on," Mom said.

I tried to swallow hard, but there was no saliva left in my mouth. My teeth kinda felt stuck to my lips. I grabbed for a glass of water on the coffee table. I couldn't hear a sound, except for my ridiculous gulp.

"I didn't want to be nosy, but the email was right in front of my face. It was from someone named Drew Edwards."

"What did it say?" Fawn asked.

I could feel sweat droplets forming on my nose. "I don't remember exactly. He mentioned that Eric was in trouble, and that he didn't like Flip very much. He also said that he didn't want Fawn getting hurt."

"Sounds like Drew. He hates pretty much everyone except Fawn." Flip turned to me. "Why didn't you say something about the email?"

I looked over in Mom's direction, but then looked away because she was glaring at me with her lips pressed tightly together and gathered at the side. I don't know how she does that.

I grabbed a napkin from the coffee table and wiped off my nose.

"Well ..." That's when I didn't know what to say. I shook my head. I didn't want to get Flip in trouble.

"Honey, if you knew someone was threatening Flip and Fawn, why wouldn't you say anything?" I think Dad could tell I was confused.

Flip interrupted and saved me. "Riley, I never saw that email. What happened to it?"

"I don't know. I left it in your inbox. You said you were going to take care of it."

"I said that?"

"Yes. In the kitchen. In the morning, before our boat ride."

Mom held her hands up in a "time-out" position. "Whoa. You two had a discussion about this email from Drew?"

"No," Flip said.

"Yes, we did."

"No, we didn't. The email we talked about was the one you sent to TJ about finding Rusty's mom."

I wadded up my napkin and squeezed it tight in my

good hand. "That's not the one I was talking about. I deleted that one."

"You didn't delete it."

"Yes, I did."

Fawn threw her arms up. "Well, I'm totally confused."

"Everyone stay put," Flip said. "Don't say a thing. I'll be right back."

I'm glad Flip suggested we all remain silent. I didn't think I could stand any more questioning.

Thankfully, Flip returned in a quick minute. He had his laptop with him.

"*This* is the email I was talking about." Flip read my email to TJ out loud. Mom's lips stayed tight, but scrunched to the other side of her mouth.

"Oh." I gulped a lump of water. "I guess I didn't delete it then. But I know I hit the delete button ..."

Flip held up his index finger. "Okay! Now we're getting somewhere." He placed that same finger onto his touch pad and clicked the arrow on the deleted file folder.

"Here it is! An email from our dear friend, Drew Edwards."

Everyone, except me, crowded around the computer.

Mom jumped up. "I've got to get some security out here." She flew out of the room with her phone.

"Maybe Eric's on the run," Fawn said. "It does say he's in trouble."

Flip shook his head. "I don't think so. Think about it,

Sis. He shows up in Fresno, out of the blue. Right after my accident. Then he lies about the plane. And ..."

"And what?"

"And I think he was holding the other side of that volleyball net."

Chapter 48

The next hour was a blur. I think my pain meds were kicking in, or maybe it was the letdown from finally telling my secret about using Flip's computer. Whatever it was, I sank into the couch and barely moved. All around me there was action. Everyone had phones hanging out of their ears. As I went in and out of sleep, I heard the names Eric, Tyler, Sunday, Rusty, Flip, and even Bob Hansen, the head business guy from Swiftriver. Someone said something about a passport. I thought I heard Chuck's voice coming from another room, but I was too tired to go ask him anything about his son. How could Lucky Chuck have a bad guy for a son? And what made him bad anyway? Then I dreamed that I was a ping-pong ball in an Olympic tournament. Thankfully, I woke up from that pretty quickly. Unfortunately, the bruises were real.

"Riley, wake up." Mom shook me a little too hard.

"Owww."

"Sorry. We have to pack. We're going to Missoula tonight."

"Why?"

"It's just better that we go tonight. Go get your suitcase and pack for a couple of days." Mom pushed a button on her phone and put it up to her ear.

I rubbed my face and tried to shake the mushiness out of my brain. "We're coming back here, right?"

"Well, maybe you better pack everything. At least all your clothes. And shoes." Mom shook her head, pushed another button and shoved her phone in her pants pocket.

"Oh no, not the shoes. There's too many."

"I'll get Rusty to help you. She and her dad are coming too." Mom started to whisper. "We're telling them that Sunday's bone marrow transplant has been moved up so we have to see him tomorrow. We reserved hotel rooms near the hospital. Come on, let's go."

"I'm sleepy." I stood up and then sat back down. "And dizzy."

"You'll be okay. Just stand up slowly. I'll go get you some juice."

Mom scurried away before I got a chance to argue more.

Brady walked in pulling his suitcase. "Are you packed yet? Isn't it great that we're going to surprise Sunday tomorrow?"

I stretched and shook my foggy head. "Yeah, it's super-duper."

Brady stared at me.

I stared back. "What?"

"You don't look good. Would you like me to help you pack?"

I shook my head again. Surely my brother wasn't offering to help me. Was he?

"I'll get your suitcase," he said. "What do you want me to pack first?"

I guess this *was* real. "Shoes, please. All of them."

"For a two-day trip?"

I had to play along with the story. Again. "Yes, I don't know which ones I'll want to wear."

"Okay, but you know you're overpacking."

"No doubt. That's what sisters do, you know."

"Then I'm glad I only have one."

"Yeah, lucky you."

I waited for him to finish up with a snappy comeback.

"Yes, I am pretty lucky. And I'm glad you're okay, Riley."

"What?"

"I'm glad you didn't get hurt worse today."

And off he went to pack my shoes. I pinched myself to see if I was still dreaming.

"Oww."

Nope. That was my brother, all right.

I smiled and shook my head again. "Glad I only have one."

Chapter 49

I don't remember the ride to Missoula. I don't even know how I got in my bed at the hotel. The only thing I remembered about the night was wandering around the room, with Mom's hands on my shoulders guiding me to a huge bathroom.

"I think this is bigger than my bedroom at home."

"Flip and Fawn got us the large suite."

"My hand hurts. My fingers are huge." I held them up for Mom to see.

"Oh my. I hope that's normal. I'll get you some ice."

I ended up back in bed somehow, and in the morning, my hand was laying on a baggie filled with warm water.

Rusty came in, looking all cleaned up and springy. "Dad and I already went to breakfast. I had a Belgian waffle. Want me to make you one and bring it up here to the room?"

"Sure, thanks." I snuck a look at the time. Nine o'clock. Okay, so it wasn't too late.

Mom came in from the hallway, carrying a big plastic bag. "We're leaving for the hospital in about an hour. If you want to shower, I'll need to wrap your cast up in this."

I sniffed my underarm. Yuck. I hadn't cleaned up since the river trip. "How about a bath instead?"

"Good idea. I'll get one going for you."

I sat up and checked my fingers again. They looked like fat little sausages. But they didn't hurt as much, and the color of the cast made me smile. Sunday was right. Orange is very cheery.

The bath felt great, and the Belgian waffle with strawberries and whipped cream tasted better than anything I had eaten in a long time. But it didn't totally fill me up, so I went searching for more food.

"Where are Flip and Fawn?" I asked, right before I sank my teeth into a humongous peach that I pulled out of a fruit basket on the coffee table.

"They're on their way to the hospital. They wanted to spend some time with Sunday's parents before everyone gets there. They figured you might need a little more time to wake up and get ready this morning." Mom combed through my wet tangles as I gobbled down the rest of the peach. "Wow—you're hungry."

Dad and Brady popped in the door with bags of Cheetos. "Orange food for Sunday," Brady said.

"Which will turn his fingers orange too," I said.

Brady held up *his* fingers and smiled. Apparently, he'd already eaten his own bag.

Dad grabbed Brady by the hands. "You're *not* getting into the car with those." He led my brother toward the bathroom. "We'll go get the car and meet you out front."

Mom gathered up my wet hair, pulled it into a ponytail, and then twisted it into a bun. "There!" Then she grabbed my Sole Fire running shoes. "Now, let's get these tied."

I felt like a toddler who needed her mother to get her ready for preschool. But, with one hand not working, how was I supposed to put on my own shoes? The Riley Mae Sport Collection didn't come with Velcro.

"Are we really going to *another* hospital?" I asked.

"At least it's not for you this time," Mom said. "And it will be a nice visit with Sunday. They say he's feeling pretty good today, and as it turns out, they really are going to do his bone marrow transplant tomorrow."

"Oh good, so we don't have to lie. I'm afraid I'm going to blow it one of these days."

Mom smiled. "Well, I guess I'm glad that you don't like to lie." She finished tying my shoes in double knots. "I just need a little more time, and then we can all be free of this Swiftriver mess."

I examined the shoes on my feet. "You know, I'm starting to like Swiftriver, and being the shoe-girl. I just want the bad guys to go away."

Mom stood up and stretched. "We all do. Just think about poor Flip and Fawn—hiding out all these years. And then to find out that their brother is one of them ..."

"You really think Eric's involved? He doesn't look dangerous to me. He just seems sad."

Mom grabbed her purse and a couple of jackets and led me out the door.

"Don't you worry about Eric," she said. "We'll find him, and we'll get this nonsense straightened out. For now, let's enjoy our visit with Sunday."

Chapter 50

Seeing Sunday's smile made me forget about everything except my pudgy fingers. That's because I was reminded of them when I held out my hand to show him my orange cast.

"Riley Mae, you need to be more careful. Girls will never buy shoes if they think they come with broken bones!"

Everyone in the room laughed. Even the kid in the curtained area next to Sunday.

Sunday leaned over to whisper to me. "That is Joshua. He is not doing well. I try to make him laugh, and I talk to him about Jesus every night. He is very interested in the Good News."

That reminded me that I had some good news to share with Sunday. "Guess what? Rusty asked Jesus into her heart when I was playing ping-pong with Flip. Can you believe that?"

"I believe most anything when it comes to God," Sunday said. "Where is Rusty?"

"She's waiting down in the lobby with her dad. He flew in to surprise her yesterday."

"Go get her. I want to welcome a new sister in Christ!"

I looked around at the crowded room. The nurses had told us that we could only have a few in at a time, so Rusty and her dad had offered to be in the second group of visitors, along with Brady and my dad.

"I don't think we can add any more people to this room."

"We'll leave," Flip said. "We get to see this kid all the time." Flip stepped over and grabbed Fawn by the shoulder. "I heard Diane was on her way. Let's go find her."

"All of my favorite people are here," Sunday said. "We should have a party." Then he yelled over in Joshua's direction. "Joshua, we are going to have a party. Would you like to come?"

"Sure," a weak little voice said from behind the curtain.

"Good," Sunday said. "Diane will find us some ice cream if I ask her."

Visiting group number two arrived, with Rusty, her dad, my dad, and Brady with the Cheetos. Brady slapped Sunday on the arm. "Hi buddy! Look what I brought for you!"

Sunday cringed and grabbed his arm. "Hit me on the other arm, please. This one has my IV filled with orange soda pop."

"Oh, sorry," Brady said. He examined the IV bag, which actually held some orangish-red liquid. "Can you taste that?"

"No, but I am sure that is a good thing. May I have some of those Cheetos?"

"Sure!" Brady said as he tore the bag open.

Both boys crunched Cheetos like they hadn't had a thing to eat in days. Orange powder now covered Sunday's white hospital sheets and gown.

"Did they give you one with a back?" I asked.

"No," Sunday said. "Hospital garments are highly insufficient."

"Sunday," Rusty said, "this is my dad, Richard Peterson." Mr. Peterson stepped forward to shake Sunday's newly powdered hand.

"It is nice to meet you, young man. My daughter tells me that you are very brave."

"She is the brave one. She climbed out of the box to save us from Herod." Sunday turned toward Rusty. "And now I hear that you are a Christian. Soon you should be baptized!"

I laughed, remembering when Sunday jumped into the water with Diane.

"Did somebody in here order Orange Sherbet?" Diane squeezed by Brady and plopped a carton on Sunday's lap. She also leaned over and kissed him on the forehead. "I know you're the most popular kid in the world, but we can't have all your friends in here at the same time. I'm going to have to kick some of them out. You think this is a party or something?"

"Actually, it is," Sunday said.

Diane straightened up and looked at me. "How's your hand?"

"Chubby."

She crossed her eyes as she looked at my fingers. "They look just about right."

She laughed and then glanced toward Rusty and her dad.

Then she backed up a few steps—and froze.

Rusty's dad stepped forward toward Diane. "Cheryl?"

Diane gasped and put her hand over her mouth. Then she turned and ran out of the room.

Rusty looked at her Dad. "Dad?"

"I'll be right back," he said. And he ran out of the room too.

Rusty pushed her fingers into her temples and looked down at the floor. She closed her eyes and grabbed her locket. She looked like she was praying. Then she raised her head, glanced over at me, and ran out the door.

Chapter 51

Rusty, wait!"

I ran out into the hallway, but Mom stopped me. "You need to stay here. Give them some time."

"Give *who* time? What's going on?" I walked down the hall a little, far enough to see Diane, sitting on one of the chairs in the lobby crying. Mr. Peterson stood next to Rusty, his hand on her shoulder.

"Why did he call her Cheryl?" I asked.

"Riley, you need to stop staring and come back here."

But I couldn't stop staring at the woman and the girl, who I just now noticed looked very much alike. Both had auburn-colored hair and the same fair skin tone. Both were tall with an athletic build.

And now they were hugging each other.

Could it be?

"Hey!" My brother yelled out into the hallway. "Are we gonna eat this ice cream before it melts?"

"I'll get spoons," I shouted back, and I charged into

the lobby. I wanted to go join Rusty and her dad and ask Nurse Diane a few important questions.

"Slow down, girl," Mom had followed me and grabbed my shirt as I ran toward my friend. "This isn't a good time."

"But you don't understand! I've been praying for Rusty to find her mom. I just want to go talk to her."

"It's not your business right now."

"Why not?"

That's when I heard Mr. Peterson's raised voice. Actually, everyone in the lobby could probably hear it.

"Forgiveness? How can you talk about forgiveness? Do you realize what you've put me through all these years? I didn't have a wife, and Rusty didn't have a mom! We've struggled to get by, and there were times when I thought I'd lose Rusty because I couldn't provide for her. All because you left! YOU, Cheryl. You left. You left your daughter. You made your choice."

Then Mr. Peterson grabbed Rusty's arm and led her away toward the elevator. Rusty still held her locket in her hand, and she turned to look at her mom, tears streaming down her face. Diane stood there, her shoulders heaving up and down. She watched as Mr. Peterson and Rusty boarded the elevator and disappeared.

Chapter 52

It was hard to think about going back into Sunday's hospital room. He was expecting a party, and he deserved one. The kid was about to have a bone marrow transplant, and yet he was the most cheerful person in the whole hospital. So I made myself go find the spoons I had promised, and I also found a smile before I walked into his room.

"Is everything okay with Diane and Rusty?" he asked, while he spooned big orange glops of sherbet into his mouth.

"Yes," I said. "God answered a prayer for them."

"I am so happy," he said. "Today is full of good news."

Flip and Fawn came back in the room, this time with Sunday's parents, Kiano and Ajia, and Sunday's three sisters, Faith, Grace, and Hope.

Little Hope jumped onto Sunday's bed. "Yum, ice cream!"

Now I knew we had too many people in the room.

"Riley," Sunday asked, "Please pull open Joshua's curtains. He is welcome to join."

I didn't know if I was allowed to do that, but hey, we were going to get into trouble anyway as soon as a nurse walked in. So I figured, why not? I grabbed the edge of the curtain and walked it around the bed where Joshua lay, hooked to all kinds of strange machines. A kid with no hair and black circles under his eyes grinned at me.

"Hey, you're that shoe-girl from the magazine," he said. I noticed on his end table that he had an *Outdoor Teen Magazine*, and it was open to *Girl vs. Rock*. "When I get well, I'm going to climb Half Dome like you did."

Kiano came over to speak with Joshua. "Yes, you can climb that mountain, no problem. I will pray that God will make it so." Then he smiled that huge Kiano smile that comes from inside.

Joshua pointed to my hand. "What happened?"

"Oh, uh ... a little collision with a rock when I was river rafting. You'll probably read about it in the next issue." I looked around at the IV bags that hung above his head, and all of a sudden my hand being broken didn't seem like such a big deal.

"That sounds kind of exciting." Joshua smiled. "What are you gonna do next?"

I shrugged. "I'd actually like to go home and start the eighth grade."

Joshua scrunched up his nose. "That sounds boring."

"I think she should train to run a long distance race," Kiano said. "What do you think, Joshua?"

Again, somebody mentioned me running more than just bases during a softball game. "What are you talking about? I don't know anything about running."

"I've offered to take you all on a trip to Kenya," Kiano said. "My people can teach you how to run."

Well, I just about fell over.

But Joshua sat up a little straighter. "Wow. Isn't that in Africa? Are they going to do another article about you in the magazine?

Kiano winked at me and then turned to Joshua. "The project is still in the planning stages."

"Yeah, and I have a broken hand," I said. "Plus, Africa is ... far."

"Yes." Kiano smiled.

By this time, Grace and Hope were jumping around me and tugging on my clothes.

"You can sleep in our bed, and we can play kickball!" Hope jumped a little too close to my hand.

"Oww."

"I am sorry, Riley." Grace grabbed her little sister away from me.

Hope frowned and looked down. "I did not mean to."

I patted her on the shoulder. "It's okay. It's just that my hand is still a little sore."

"Will it feel better when you are at our house?" Hope rubbed my cast.

"I guess that depends on when we're going to your house."

"I hope you go soon," Joshua said. "I want to read more articles about your adventures."

"It will be soon," Kiano said. Then he winked at me again.

Chapter 53

I needed to find a chair. And some air. Somehow, I managed to escape to a nice bench outside the hospital. Rusty had found the same one.

"Hi," I said.

"Hi." Rusty stared straight ahead at a pine tree.

"Nice tree."

"Yeah."

"Mind if I stare at it too?"

She laughed a little. "No."

So we stared for a few minutes. It was peaceful, watching the breeze play games with the pine needles. I got up and picked up a bunch and sniffed them. I brought a few back to the bench.

"I always like to braid these, but my hand's not working so well." I handed a cluster to Rusty. She braided one and handed it back to me.

"Thanks," I said.

"Riley, I'm really confused. I prayed to find my

mom, and God answered my prayer. I thought everything would be perfect if that *one* thing was right in my life, but now everything seems more messed up than before."

I didn't know what to say. "I—"

"She was *here* the whole time. She didn't even change her name; she just went by her middle name. It would have been easy for my dad to find her. Why didn't he look for her?"

"I—"

"Couldn't he have tried a *little* harder? And why didn't my mom ever come to see me? It's been so many years. You'd think that maybe on my birthday or Christmas … something!"

That's when the sobs came. I stopped trying to say something and just put my good hand on her back. I looked around and noticed that my mom was talking to Diane as they stood in the distance, watching us.

Rusty's phone rang, which made us both jump. She pulled the phone out of her pocket, looked at the screen, and then, without a word, handed it to me.

I pressed the answer button. "Hey, TJ."

"Riley, is that *you?*"

"Yep. How's it going?"

"It's going great. Are you ever coming home?"

"Don't know. I may have another photo shoot to do for running shoes."

"Running? Yuck! But that reminds me of a crazy softball play that happened the other day. We had this girl in a pickle between third and home, and you know how my dad is always saying that the perfect rundown takes no throws, but the third baseman gets all panicked and actually throws home ..."

I turned it on speaker and held it up for Rusty to hear.

"... but at least she makes a good throw, but then the catcher *misses* it—can you believe it? Luckily, I was covering, and no way am I gonna let this punky little girl score, so I scoop up the ball and dive toward her."

TJ stopped talking for a moment, but it was only to catch her breath.

"So, just as I dive in her direction, she heads back to third, but it's too late, cause I tag her, and then her shoe flies off and I somehow end up holding it in my glove along with the ball."

"Wow," I said.

"Yep, and *guess* what kind of shoe it was?"

"I—"

"You guessed it. A Riley Mae Crazy Daisy. And even though I was way excited about getting the girl out and everything, I was immediately sad because it made me miss my best friend. How come you never call or text me?"

"I'm sorry, TJ. My phone's, uh ... gone."

"Well, that stinks. The email was cool though. Did you find Rusty's mom?"

"That's kind of complicated." Rusty shook her head like she didn't want me to say anything. Then she got up and went over to join my mom and Diane.

I needed to change the subject.

"How's church? Is Sean piling up the donuts for me?"

"Oh, I haven't been to church at all since you left. I have tournaments every weekend. I *did* see Sean, though. He was out riding his bike with this new kid named Morgan. He said they've been going to youth group together on Sunday mornings instead of helping in kids' church. Oh—and this is so funny—Sean's voice is all squeaky, and I noticed a few hairs growing on his upper lip."

"You're joking."

"Ha! Maybe. But you better come home and see for yourself. School starts pretty soon, you know. Which means your birthday is coming too. Breanne says you should have a boy-girl party when you turn thirteen."

"Boys? I don't know any boys that I actually talk to, except Sean."

"Well, I know a few cute ones we could invite."

I couldn't believe I was talking about this. I didn't even know where I would be on my birthday. But I went on anyway.

"Is that new kid Morgan cute? I guess we could invite him."

"Um … well, yes, Morgan *is* very cute, but—"

241

"Not that my mom would ever let me have a boy-girl party."

"Well, with Morgan—"

"But it *would* be nice to see Sean. I guess I miss him. Don't tell *anyone* I told you that. Do you think he misses me?"

"Well, actually—"

"I'm glad at least he has Morgan to hang out with at church."

"Oh dear."

"What? Do you have to go?"

"No, it's just that—"

"What?"

"I'm not sure how to tell you this."

"You've never had trouble telling me anything before. We're best friends. Spill it."

"Uhhh—"

"Go on."

"Riley?"

"What?"

"Morgan's a girl."

Chapter 54

Rusty returned to the bench to find me staring at the tree again.

"Are you okay? You look pale." Rusty handed me her soda, and I took a long sip.

I handed her phone and her drink back to her. "Thanks. I just got the shock of my life."

"Wow—that makes both of us in one day. I guess we need to go get some chocolate."

"Okay."

We found some chocolate cookies in the hospital cafeteria. "These will do, but they're not as good as Shari Olivia cookies."

Rusty smiled. "I wish we could go back to that awesome kitchen right now and bake some." Then she looked down and frowned. "But my dad's taking me home today."

"Why? You just found your mom!"

"Yeah. He's really upset about the whole thing. He

says we need some time to think about what to do next. Diane—my mom, I mean—agrees. She says she's going to arrange her schedule so she can come out and visit in a few weeks. My dad wants her to sign divorce papers."

"What?"

"I know, weird, huh? My parents are still married after all this time."

Chapter 55

Before I could go back into the hospital to visit with Sunday, I had to go to the lab where they gave me shots.

"Is this torture necessary?" I asked Mom.

Mom sighed real big. That usually means that she's trying to figure out how to give me bad news.

"Well, we might be going on another trip, so you need to be immunized. Actually we're all getting shots."

Mom grimaced as the nurse thrust a needle in her arm. "We've got the authorities out looking for Eric, but if they don't find him soon then we have to get out of sight for a while. He knows where we all live and where all the Stevens' hideouts are."

"Kiano mentioned something about Africa," I grabbed Mom's sleeve. "Please tell me we're not going there."

Mom put her hand on my shoulder and looked into my eyes. "We'll see, Honey. Kiano assured us that the people in his village can watch out for us and keep us safe, and that's the most important thing right now. "

Flip and Fawn came into the lab to join us.

"I'll have what she's having," Flip said, as he rolled up his sleeves for his shots.

"I'm tired of hospitals," I said.

"Well, you're in luck, because there aren't too many where we're going."

"You mean where we *might* be going."

"Awe, c'mon shoe-girl, where's your sense of adventure? Don't you wanna ride an elephant or something?" Flip watched as the nurse pushed three needles into his arm. "YOUCH! Give a guy a break, will ya?"

Fawn laughed and shook her head. "You poor baby. Here, watch how it's done." Fawn rolled up her sleeves and smiled the whole time while the nurse gave her three shots. Then she hugged the nurse. "Thanks for doing that. I know it's not easy doing your job when you have such whiners all the time."

Dad and Brady joined us, but didn't get shots. "If you guys want to see Sunday, you ought to go now. The nurses want him to get some rest for tomorrow's procedure."

Only I went. Flip and Fawn said they had just been up to visit, and Mom stopped short in the hallway to Sunday's room. "I think he might like to talk to you alone," she said.

When I walked in the room, Sunday was sleeping. Joshua's curtain was closed, so I wasn't even sure if he was in the room.

I plunked down on the chair next to Sunday's bed. I dropped my head back and stared up at the white tiles of the hospital ceiling. Then I closed my eyes. It was peaceful in here, but that didn't make sense. A kid with cancer lay next to me with all kinds of stuff hooked up to him, about to go in for a serious operation that might save his life, but maybe not. My hand was in a cast, caused by some bad guys who obviously didn't care if a whole raft of people plunged down a treacherous water-fall. My friend Rusty found her mom, which turned out to be a disaster. And I might be traveling to Africa, of all places, and I didn't know if I'd ever return home again.

And Morgan's a *girl* ...

"Is that you, Riley Mae?"

I opened my eyes to see Sunday, squinting in my direction.

"I think so."

Sunday sat up. "What do you mean by that? Do you not know?"

"Well, it *is* me. But, I don't know. I'm different these days. Not the same Riley Mae who started all this shoe business a few months ago."

"Of course you are different. Each day, we all are different. God is growing us. That is a good thing."

"It doesn't feel like a good thing." I pointed to Sunday's IV hookup. "How can *this* be a good thing for you?"

"Sometimes it seems bad. And sometimes it is very

painful. But I know that it causes me to cling to God. He is always here with me. We talk together. I love him. I think I might ignore him otherwise."

"I guess that makes sense. I've been talking to God a lot lately."

"You see, that is what he wants."

A familiar, squeaky noise sounded outside the room. In walked a pair of nurses, wheeling Joshua in his bed.

"Hello, my friend," Sunday said. "How was it?"

"Not so bad this time," Joshua said.

"I prayed for that." Sunday grinned.

I decided not to ask what they were talking about.

"Your dad wants us all to go to Africa." I looked at Sunday and shook my head. "Is that crazy, or what?"

Sunday put his fist up to his chin. "I think it is a good plan. You would like the animals, the color of the sunsets, and all the friendly children."

"Yeah, but what about the food?"

"It is good! Especially Chapati."

"What's that?"

Sunday rubbed his stomach. "Delicious flatbread!"

"But Africa is such a long way from home."

"I am a long way from home, and I am fine."

I looked around at all the machines and dripping bags in the hospital room. "Well, okay, if you say so."

Sunday took a sip of water and nodded. "Do you know what I like best about my village? The people love God very much. They do not have a lot of things. But they have him."

"That sounds nice."

"You would feel at home with them."

He laid back and pulled his blanket up to his chin, and his feet popped out from the bottom. Well, it wasn't his bare feet. He was wearing the orange running shoes. I laughed. "You never take those things off, do you?"

Sunday smiled. "They are special. Flip gave them to me the day he came to take me to the United States for my cancer treatments. That was a very good day for me."

"So, you don't just wear them because they're orange?"

"No. But that will be our secret. I also like the new name—Sole Fire. It reminds me that I want my soul to be on fire for God—no matter what."

I wanted to ask Sunday what he meant by that, but Diane came in. It looked like her face was red from crying. "I have to steal you for one more test, Buddy." Then she turned to me. "He'll need his rest after that, Riley, so you should probably say good-bye now."

I gave Sunday a hug.

"Say hello to everyone in Kenya for me," he said.

"Very funny. I'm probably not even going."

"Tell them that I am getting better, and I will be home soon."

"Sunday, you're not even listening to me, are you?"

He laughed a little, and Diane helped him and all his IV bags transfer from the bed to a wheelchair. Then she reached over and gave me a hug. "Thanks for bringing my daughter to Montana."

"You're welcome, but I'm pretty sure it was God that brought you guys together."

As Diane wheeled Sunday out, he pointed to me and smiled. "See you soon, Riley Mae. Enjoy your Sole Fire Safari!" Then he laughed that crazy Sunday laugh, and he was gone.

I laughed too. I couldn't help it. But how could he joke at a time like this? Going to Africa right now sounded like the most ridiculous idea on the planet. What I really wanted was for *him* to go home to Africa, and for me to take all my Riley Mae outdoor shoes right back to Fresno, where they belonged. That would be the best plan, right?

Go against the flow, Riley.

I slumped back on the chair and blew out my breath real hard. I crossed my arms and rested them on Sunday's bed and laid my head down on top of them. My eyes focused down on my feet.

Once again, I thought of that Bible verse from Ephesians, chapter six:

"For shoes, put on the peace that comes from the Good News so that you will be fully prepared."

Yeah, but ... prepared for *what*?

A Sunday school song popped into my head, and I

could almost hear little Ava Zimmer from children's church singing it:

"I've got peace like a river, I've got peace like a river, I've got peace like a river in my soul ..."

And that made me sit up and laugh out loud, since a river almost swept me over a fifteen foot waterfall. I sure wasn't prepared for that!

I remembered the eddy, and how I tried to swim to it by myself, but all I managed to do was thrash around and be pulled closer to the falls. The only reason I made it there safely was because of Matt. Thankfully he'd been thrown into the river too, which made it easier for him to save me. Dad would probably call that a "God Moment." And he'd be right. In fact, when I really thought about it, I realized that God had been protecting me throughout this whole Swiftriver adventure. Okay, so maybe I ended up with a broken hand, some cuts, and a bruised-up lip from that silly ping-pong ball, but those things had started me talking to God more, and—like Sunday said—that meant I was growing closer to him, right?

So, could it be that God was using all these things to prepare me to take these "Good News Shoes" to Africa?

Hmm ... maybe. Definitely maybe.

But I sure hoped NOT!

So I prayed real hard, and I punched the pillow too:

Dear God, thanks for taking care of me and my family and

friends. And thank you that Rusty asked you into her heart, and that she found her mom. Please help the police find Eric and Drew before they hurt anyone else. And please help me be a better spokesgirl for Swiftriver and also to share the Good News of Jesus—like maybe with Fawn. And please let me go back home to Fresno.

Tomorrow.

That's all for now.

Amen.

We want to hear from you. Please send your comments about this book to us in care of zreview@zondervan.com. Thank you.